BETWEEN PRO[ ] AND BIN[ ]
BEING THIN WITHOU[ ] [ ]SSIONS

This is a work of fiction. Similarities to real people, places, or events are entirely coincidental.

BETWEEN PROHIBITIONS AND BINGES

First edition. November 11, 2024.

Copyright © 2024 Mauricio Aban.

ISBN: 979-8227755599

Written by Mauricio Aban.

MAURICIO ABAN

Chapter 1:

It's funny how memories from school can haunt you, even when you think you're over it. No matter how much I change or how hard I try, there are things that are still there, like scars that neither time nor words can erase. I look in the mirror and recognize the reflection of someone who struggled, but behind that clean, skinny image, I can still see the fat, clumsy kid who hid in bathrooms to avoid stares.

"Why are you so quiet, Tyler?" they would say, mockingly.

The question haunts me to this day. It was easier to stay silent, hoping they would pass me by, forget about me even for a few minutes. I became a ghost in my own life. I never answered because I knew any word from me would only give them more weapons. So I learned not to speak.

I remember Ben, always the ringleader of the mockery. "Fat Tyler," "Sad Pig," "You ate more than Grandma's lunch again, huh?" It was like they had created a language especially to destroy me, a language that no one else seemed to understand or hear. Just me. The worst part was that everyone seemed to laugh, even the ones who didn't want to get involved. Their laughter still haunts me.

"Come on, Tyler, why don't you run?" Ben would say during gym class.

My chest ached every time I tried. Every word, every laugh was like a punch to the stomach, and I still wonder if they ever imagined the damage they were causing me.

I will never forget the day I hid in the bathroom and heard the door open. I wanted to disappear at that moment, but my legs wouldn't respond. I was still trying to calm my breathing when I heard Megan's voice.

"Oh, poor Tyler, he should be ashamed of himself for even coming to school in that body," he said, not knowing I was there, not knowing that every word he said was pushing me one step closer to the abyss.

One day I gathered my courage, tried to look her in the eyes and said:

—You have no idea how I feel.

His reaction was immediate, a mixture of surprise and disgust.

"What makes you think I care, Tyler?" she replied coldly.

That night I lay awake, staring at the ceiling, hearing his words over and over in my head. "What makes you think I care?" That phrase stuck with me, and I still repeat it to myself in those moments when I'm trying to find a reason to get up. I never wanted to care so much, but for some reason, his approval, or any of theirs, became something I desperately wanted.

Sometimes in my dreams, I see myself walking through the halls, but I'm no longer alone. Instead of laughing, my classmates look at me with admiration, as if I were finally someone worth seeing. But those dreams fade when I wake up, and the harsh reality returns me to the same reflection in the mirror: a reflection I barely recognize, someone who has changed so much physically that others would barely recognize me.

I struggle to remember the reason for all this sacrifice. The reason I lost the weight, why I changed. Was it for them? Was it for me? The answer evades me, because if I'm honest with myself, I don't know if this transformation made me happier.

That same afternoon, while I was looking through old photos on my phone, I found one from high school. There I was, standing in the corner, trying to disappear. My eyes were full of fear, and something inside me broke at the look on my face. I wondered what he would think of me if he saw me now, if he would be proud of what I accomplished, or disappointed that, despite everything, I still feel like an intruder in my own body.

My mother came into the room at that moment. She had noticed that I had been staying away from family meals, and although she seemed relieved at first about my weight loss, there was now a concern she couldn't hide.

"Tyler, honey, are you okay?" she asked, her voice filled with concern.

"Yes, Mom," I replied, but the tone sounded hollow even to my own ears.

She came closer and looked at me with a mixture of sadness and guilt. Maybe because she knew that, at some point, she had also contributed to this, without even realizing it. In her attempts to make me fit in, she constantly reminded me of the importance of looking "good." It was a subtle message, disguised as love, but just as damaging.

—I don't want you to lose yourself, son, —he whispered.

I felt my heart stop. "Losing myself." Wasn't it too late for that? I had spent years trying to find myself, trying to become someone other than the one they saw. I had changed my appearance, I had built a mask that could hide what I really felt. But despite everything, I still felt lost.

"Don't worry, Mom," I finally said. "I'm fine."

She didn't insist any further and left. However, her words hung in the air, like a reminder that, no matter how hard I tried to run away, there were still parts of me that I couldn't erase.

After he left, I looked at myself in the mirror again. The high cheekbones, the thin face, and the eyes that once sparkled with a spark of hope now seemed dark, dull. I wondered if they saw me differently now, if Ben, Megan, or any of those who hurt me would recognize me, or if I would just be another face in the crowd.

Maybe I would never know, but one thing was certain: I was no longer the same, and although that should make me feel better, the truth is that it made me feel emptier than ever.

I turned away from the mirror, letting darkness fill the room. I had achieved what I wanted, or so I thought, but the question continued to haunt me. Who did I really do it for? For them, who didn't even think about the damage they caused? Or for me, who at some point stopped caring enough to lose myself in this attempt to be someone I could never be?

In the silence of the night, a lone tear slid down my cheek.

Chapter 2:

There are moments in life that remain etched in memory. For some, they are happy memories, days of laughter with friends or endless adventures. For me, those moments are others: the whispers, the looks of contempt, the chuckles, and the comments that pierced like needles every school day.

Every morning before I left the house, I tried to convince myself that today would be different. I silently told myself that it didn't matter what they thought, that I could ignore them and that soon this would all be over. But once I was in the classroom, my courage crumbled.

"Look, here comes Tyler, you better make room!" Ben said in his loud, mocking voice as everyone else laughed.

I tried not to look at them, to pretend I wasn't listening, but they always found a way to make sure every word, every laugh, hit me like a knife. I sat in the back, trying to make myself small, to disappear, but that only seemed to make things worse.

—Hey, Tyler, how many burgers did you eat today? —one of the boys asked with a laugh.

I didn't answer. I knew that anything I said would only add fuel to the fire.

—Oh, of course, I'm sure he doesn't want to tell us. There must have been about twenty of them, right? —another insisted.

It was a question that made no sense to answer. It wasn't true, but somehow I didn't even know why it affected me so much. I just felt a knot in my stomach, a burning in my chest, and a desperate need to escape.

I remember one time in the dining hall, one day I tried to work up the courage to sit at one of the tables. I thought that if I acted confidently, maybe they would stop making me feel like an intruder. But not even a minute had passed when I heard laughter all around me.

"Tyler, what are you doing here?" Megan asked, looking at me with contempt. "That chair is going to break if you sit on it."

Her friends' laughter was so loud that I felt like all eyes were on me, like I was on a stage and they were the audience, waiting for me to make the next mistake. I gulped, trying to ignore her, but Megan stepped even closer.

"Did you hear what I told you, Tyler?" she insisted, her voice laced with venom. "We don't want to see you here, so why don't you just go and eat alone, like always?"

My body was stiff, my hands were sweating, and an unpleasant heat was rising up my neck. Everything in me was screaming for me to get up and leave, but there was something inside that wanted to stand firm, not wanting to give them the pleasure of seeing me run again.

"Leave him alone, Megan," a girl sitting nearby murmured.

"What? You feel sorry for him now?" Megan replied with a grimace. "You don't need to do that, believe me, he's used to it."

Finally, my feet caught up and I stood up, my heart beating so fast it felt like it was going to jump out of my chest. I walked toward the door without looking back, but I knew they were watching me, and as I walked out, I heard Megan's laughter. That sound stuck in my mind, like an echo I couldn't shake.

I found myself taking refuge in the bathrooms more and more often, closing the door of one of the stalls and sitting on the floor, counting the minutes until the nightmare would end. But even there I was not safe. One day, while I was locked in the stall, I heard someone enter and recognized the voices of Ben and his group.

"Tyler, are you hiding again?" one of them shouted, while the others laughed and banged on the door.

"Come on, little pig, are you scared?" Ben said mockingly. "Why don't you come out? We promise not to hit you... well, maybe just a little."

Their laughter was cruel, but worse was the feeling of being trapped. I knew that if I left, I would be humiliated in front of everyone who passed by in the hallway, and if I stayed, they would continue to harass me until they got bored. So I stayed silent, trembling, waiting for them to get tired and leave.

"Are you crying, Tyler?" one of them asked, as if they actually cared.

I bit my lip, feeling the tears begin to slide down my cheeks. I knew that if I answered, they would only laugh harder. I wanted to tell them to stop, that there was nothing wrong with being who I was, but my words stuck in my throat.

Finally, after what seemed like hours, I heard them leaving, laughing and mumbling amongst themselves. I waited a few minutes before leaving and looked at myself in the bathroom mirror. My face was pale, and my eyes were swollen and red. That was the reflection of someone defeated, someone who no longer had the strength to continue fighting.

I sometimes wonder what would have happened if I had asked for help. If I had told a teacher or my parents what was going on. But I couldn't, because I felt a deep shame, a sense that I was the problem, that they were right to treat me this way because I didn't fit in. How could I explain to them what I felt without them laughing even more?

That night, as I tried to sleep, I heard the voices in my head. The taunts, the laughter, every hurtful word. It was like a part of me had broken and I didn't know how to fix it anymore. I wondered if I would ever change, if one day they would look at me and see someone worthy of respect.

But deep down, I knew the truth: They would never see me any other way. To them, I would always be Tyler the Pig, the fat kid, the easy joke. And that thought consumed me, made me feel like I was trapped in an endless nightmare from which I could never wake up.

That was one of the last times I stayed in the school cafeteria or tried to defend myself. Little by little, I began to disappear, to become a ghost who was just passing through. I stopped trying to fit in, I stopped talking and looking people in the eye.

Now, when I close my eyes, I can remember every word as if they were being said right now. Every taunt lives on inside me, and even if I try hard to forget them, those voices don't go away. They're there, reminding me of who I was and, in some ways, who I still am.

Those words became my shadow, the weight I carry with me every day. And even though I changed my appearance, even though I became someone different, I can't help but feel that deep down, I'm still that scared boy, hiding in the bathroom, trembling, while the laughter and murmurs continue in my head, like a wound that never heals.

Chapter 3:

I don't know when it started, but there came a time when I felt that cruelty was not only coming from school, but also from home. Instead of finding refuge, my home became another place I feared returning to. Not because it was physical, but because every word, every comment, was a thorn that reminded me of how little I was worth.

One night at dinner, my parents talked about me as if I wasn't there. Mom started laughing as she told a story about when I was younger and apparently "chubbier."

"Remember, honey?" she said to Dad with a smile. "Tyler always asked for double portions at dinner. I don't know how he did it, but he was able to eat everyone's dessert. He was a glutton!"

I felt the color rise in my cheeks. I knew I was about to hear another story about when I was "the fat kid" of the family. Even though my mother tried to say it as a joke, the weight of her words fell on me like a burden I couldn't shake.

Dad laughed and shook his head.

—Of course I remember. And look at him now, where did all that "affection" go? —he said, looking me up and down, as if analyzing my body was an entertaining show.

I sat there silently, pushing the food around on my plate, feeling like a stranger in my own home. The mockery was constant, and though I tried to ignore it, each comment dug deeper, like small wounds that never healed.

But it wasn't just at dinner. Any time was an excuse to remember how inadequate I was, how disappointing I seemed to be to them. My aunt, whenever she came to visit, couldn't help but comment on my weight, my habits, or what she considered "my faults." Sometimes, she even tried to make jokes about it.

"Tyler, you should learn to eat like your cousins," she once said, looking at me with a smile that hid contempt. "They have no problem controlling what they eat. Maybe that's why they're so athletic and not... well, like you."

My mother's gaze shifted uncomfortably, but she didn't say anything. She just shrugged and muttered:

—Tyler was always... different.

"Different." That word haunted me all my life. They said I was different, but never in a tone that sounded like something good. Being "different" to them meant failure, a silent disappointment. No one bothered to hide it too much; it seemed like, for them, making me feel like an outsider was normal, as if they were used to seeing me suffer without doing anything.

I remember one night in particular. We were at my cousin's birthday party, surrounded by family, when I was served a piece of cake. I felt all eyes on me, as if they were waiting to see how much I would eat. I tried to act normal, to ignore their eyes on me, but then I heard my aunt's low laugh.

"Tyler, don't be such a greedy person," she said through clenched teeth, though everyone could hear her. "We have to leave some for the others, okay?"

Some of the cousins laughed, and my father just gave me a reproachful look before saying, mockingly:

—That's it, Tyler, control yourself a bit. We don't want you to be a ball again.

The word "ball" echoed in my mind, louder than I would like. My hands began to shake, and I felt my eyes filling with tears. I tried hard not to let them fall, but anger and pain boiled inside me. At that moment, I wished I could disappear, be invisible, stop being the focus of those judgmental stares.

Finally, I put down my fork and stood up from the table. Silence fell for a second, but Mom just smiled as if nothing had happened.

"Oh, don't be so sensitive, Tyler," she said, throwing her hands up in a playful gesture. "We're just playing."

I stared at her, wanting to scream at her that this wasn't a joke, that every word she said hurt more than I could ever imagine. But what good would it do? If I told them how I felt, they would just laugh harder or tell me I was exaggerating, that it wasn't that bad.

I left the room, my chest tight, and locked myself in the bathroom. When I looked in the mirror, the reflection I saw was that of someone I no longer recognized. It was as if those comments, those words, had deformed me into someone I hated. I saw in my eyes the shadow of that sad child, whom everyone pointed out for his weight, and for the first time, I understood that they had taught me to hate myself.

I heard footsteps and knocks on the door.

—Tyler, come on out now, it's not that big of a deal —my father said from outside, sighing—. It's just a joke, you don't have to make a big deal out of everything.

I didn't answer. If I opened my mouth, I knew all that would come out would be a muffled scream, a plea from someone who no longer knew how to ask for help. I wanted to tell them to stop, to understand what I was feeling, but I was stuck in that cycle, in that dynamic that would never change.

Finally, I returned to my room and fell onto the bed. I covered my face with my hands and let the tears fall. At some point, the words of my aunt, my father, all of them, mixed in my head until they formed an unbearable chorus. "Greedy." "Ball." "Watch what you eat." "You were always different."

I closed my eyes and swore that one day I would be free of those words, of that weight I felt on my chest. That I would look in the mirror and see something different. That I would no longer be marked by the judgments of others. But deep down, a part of me knew that they had gotten into my mind, that it was no longer possible to forget their words, even if I tried.

From that night on, I avoided looking in the mirror as much as I could. Every time I did, I saw that "ball" they talked about. I couldn't help it. My own eyes gave me back that look of contempt they had taught me. I began to believe that maybe they were right, that maybe I was what they said I was.

The irony is that they don't know it. They don't know that they've become my inner voice, that cruel reflection I see every time I have the courage to look at myself. They don't know that by making fun of me, they've taken away a part of me that I can never get back.

Chapter 4:

My father's words are like a knife that, with each comment, sinks a little deeper into me. It cuts me so deeply that I can't help but feel trapped, immobilized, as if I were a statue created only to receive his scorn. But no, he doesn't see that; to him, I'm the problem, and the more he looks at me, the more flaws he seems to find.

"Tyler, have you ever looked in the mirror?" he asks me one night, frowning as he leans in. "That acne... God, it's disgusting. Don't you know how to take care of yourself?"

I don't dare look him in the eye. I stay still, trying to disappear, hoping that if I don't answer, maybe he'll tire and leave me alone. But he doesn't give up that easily. He crosses his arms, his eyes fixed on me, his expression full of disappointment.

—On top of your weight, you also have that pimple-covered face now. How do you expect people to respect you like that? —she continues, as if her words weren't harsh enough already—. You look terrible, Tyler. I can't understand why you don't do anything to change that.

I want to shout at him that I'm trying, that I'm trying to improve every day, but the words get stuck in my throat. Instead, I nod slowly, feeling the self-hatred grow with every passing second. And deep down, a part of me is starting to believe that he's right, that I'm just as horrible as he says.

That night, after he leaves, I lock myself in the bathroom and stare at myself in the mirror. The cold bathroom lights reflect off my face, illuminating every blemish, every scar I've left on my skin from picking at pimples. I can see the redness on my face, the uneven texture, and my father's words echo in my mind, as if he were still there, behind me, watching me with contempt.

Without thinking, I bring my hands up to my face and start squeezing one of the pimples on my cheek. I feel a sharp pain as pus and blood ooze out, but it's a pain I've grown accustomed to. It's like every time I hurt myself, I'm punishing myself for being who I am, for not being good enough, for being ugly.

"What are you doing?" I ask myself quietly, almost not wanting to listen to myself.

But I don't stop. My fingers keep moving, searching for the next pimple, the next blemish I can pick out. Sometimes I imagine that if I can just get rid of all the pimples, if I can just erase every blemish, then he'll stop. Maybe one day he'll look at me and see something he likes, something he can accept.

My hands shake as I continue, fingers sliding across my skin searching for more imperfections, each squeeze leaving red marks and blood staining my fingers. It's a self-destructive ritual, something I do almost without thinking, as if my hands had a life of their own, as if they knew better than I how to erase this ugliness.

"God, Tyler, look what you've done to your face," my mother said to me one morning when she saw me coming out of the bathroom, my face red and swollen after a night of trying to "clean" my face. Her words, while not as harsh as my father's, hurt just as much. There was a mix of pity and revulsion in her voice that made the pain spread like poison inside me.

I didn't answer. I had nothing to say to him, because I already knew what he was thinking. They had made it clear long ago: I was a disappointment, a burden, someone who would never be enough. And as hard as I tried to convince myself that wasn't true, I found it increasingly difficult.

The days went by, and every time my father looked at me, it was like he found a new reason to despise me. There were days when he would tell me that my acne was my fault for not taking care of myself, for being "a creep"; other days he would focus on my weight, and then look at me with disgust, saying:

—You know, Tyler, maybe you're just not meant to be an attractive person. Some people just aren't, and you... well, you're one of them.

Those words echoed in my head over and over again. "You're not meant to be attractive." They were such cold words, so merciless, and yet he made them sound like he was speaking an obvious truth. After hearing them, I would walk up the stairs in silence, my chest tight and my eyes filled with tears that I refused to let out. Because I knew that crying wouldn't change anything, that he would still see me the same way.

One night, while I was alone in my room, I looked at myself in the small mirror on my desk. My reflection gave me an image that I found difficult to accept. The face marked by the scars I had created myself, the redness of my skin and the tired eyes that looked at me sadly. I felt an intense rage rising inside me, a rage directed at myself, at that face that I could not stop seeing as a curse.

"Why are you like this?" I whispered to myself, with a mixture of disgust and despair. "Why can't you be... normal?"

My fingers moved back to my face, and once again I began to squeeze. This time, without any control, without any intention of stopping. I wanted to tear off my skin, to erase every piece of that person I hated so much. I felt that if I could just make those pimples, those scars, disappear, then maybe, just maybe, my father would look at me with some respect.

I lost track of time, and when I finally stopped, my face was swollen, red, and bleeding. I looked in the mirror, but the reflection I saw wasn't my own. It was the reflection of someone broken, someone who could no longer recognize themselves. And in that moment, I understood that I might never be able to see anything different in the mirror.

I staggered out of the bathroom and made my way to my bed. I let myself fall and closed my eyes, trying to ignore the burning on my skin, the echo of my father's words still ringing in my head. I wanted to sleep,

I wanted to escape this torment that seemed to have no end, but I knew that tomorrow, it would all start again. I knew my father would look at me, find a new flaw, a new reason to make me feel like I didn't deserve to exist.

And as I lay in the darkness of my room, my face in pain and my heart broken, I knew there was no escape. This was my life, my reality, and all I could do was endure the pain and wait, even though I didn't know what I was waiting for.

I was hoping... maybe, one day, to wake up and see something different about myself.

Chapter 5:

The classroom feels like a cell. Every time I walk in, I know it's going to be another day of whispered comments, laughter behind my back, and stares studying me as if I'm a spectacle for their entertainment. My classmates always seem to find something new to criticize; today it's my acne, tomorrow my weight, the day after... I don't know, but they always find something.

Ever since I started gaining weight and acne began covering my face, my life has become an endless series of humiliations. I try to get to class without attracting attention, I sit in the back row, but it seems that no matter how hard I try to make myself invisible, I'm always there, an easy target for them.

Today, as I'm quietly taking notes, I feel like someone is watching me. I look up and see Ryan, one of the popular kids, staring at me with a disgusted smile.

—Hey, Tyler, —he says loudly, so everyone can hear—, have you ever thought about washing your face? I mean, do you like looking so... dirty?

The others laugh, and I look down, clenching the pen in my hands. I don't want to answer him, knowing that anything I say will only make things worse. But Ryan doesn't stop.

—Seriously, bro, that face... looks like a minefield —he continues, eliciting another laugh from the group surrounding him.

I swallow my words and pretend to concentrate on the notebook, even though I'm not writing anything. I focus on my hands, on my breathing, trying to block out their laughter. However, shame invades me, runs through me like poison. I feel the sweat beginning to form on my forehead, as if my own body wants to betray me at the most inopportune moment.

And then someone else, a girl in front, turns to me and wrinkles her nose.

BETWEEN PROHIBITIONS AND BINGES 19

"Anybody else smell it?" she says with a grimace of disgust. "Tyler, have you ever heard the word 'deodorant'?"

The laughter is louder now, and I feel my skin burning, the heat rising to my face and the sweat starting to break out even more. I try to cover myself, but I know it's useless. I can smell my sweat, the mix of nerves and embarrassment that suffocates me. And even though I know I showered before coming to school, I start to doubt. Maybe they're right, maybe I do smell bad, maybe I'm... disgusting.

—Seriously, Tyler, it smells like crap every time you walk in there, another guy adds, laughing.

I want to scream at them that they're wrong, that it's not true. But the words get stuck in my throat. Deep inside, something inside me is starting to believe that they're right, that I really am repulsive, that every single thing they say about me is true.

At the end of class, I try to leave quickly, but not quickly enough to avoid a group of boys blocking my way. Ryan is in the middle, with that arrogant smile that I hate so much.

"Where are you going so fast, you stinker?" he asks me, laughing. Some of his friends pat him on the back, encouraging him to keep going. "Are you afraid to stay here with us? Don't worry, we just want to help you."

One of the guys pulls a spray deodorant out of his backpack and throws it at me, as if it were a piece of trash he's getting rid of.

—For you to wear, bro —he tells me, and laughter breaks out again in the group.

I look at the deodorant on the floor and want to tell them to shut up, to leave me alone, but I know that if I do, they'll only make things worse. So I duck my head and walk past them, feeling their laughter pierce my spine like needles. Each laugh is a reminder of how worthless I am, how disgusting they see me.

I lock myself in the bathroom, letting the silence envelop me. Solitude is my only refuge, the only place where I can allow myself to drop my façade. I approach the mirror and look at my reflection. My face is red, marked by pimples, sweat still glistening on my forehead. I run my hand over my skin and feel the pain, the discomfort of a skin I no longer recognize.

"Why am I like this?" I whisper to myself, not expecting an answer.

Deep down, I know there is no answer. I've tried everything, used every cream I can get my hands on, showered until my skin is dry, and still, nothing changes. They still see me as a monster, and every day it's harder for me not to see it too.

The bathroom door slams open, and one of the guys walks in, gives me a disgusted look, and laughs.

—I knew you'd be here, hiding, like always. Why don't you just go out and face it, Tyler? It's not that hard... although, well, for you it probably is. It must be hard to live with the knowledge that no one can stand to be around you.

He looks me up and down, with an expression of mocking pity.

"You know what?" he says as he walks away. "I think the problem is that you suck yourself. Maybe you just can't do anything about it. Maybe you're always going to be like this."

And with those words, he walks away, leaving me alone in front of the mirror. I hate him. I hate all of them. But most of all, I hate myself. Because deep down, a part of me believes they're right. That I'll always be this way. That I can never change.

I look down at my hands, shaking, gripping the sink tightly until my knuckles turn white. I feel a desperation so deep it chokes me, a sadness that tangles in my chest and crushes me. I don't want to live like this, I don't want to be this person everyone despises, this thing that can't even look in the mirror without hating itself.

I run my hands over my face, trying to wipe away the tears I don't want to fall. But it's no use; the pain seeps in, drips, reminding me that in this world, I'm just a shadow, something others see and reject.

Silently, I turn around and walk out of the bathroom, feeling emptier than ever. Because I know that tomorrow will be the same. That they will be there, waiting to remind me of what I am, and that no matter how hard I try, I will never be able to escape this image they have built of me.

Maybe, deep down, that image is all I am.

Chapter 6:

It's funny how pain builds a wall around you. One day you laugh at yourself to try to go unnoticed, and the next you realize you can't remember the last time you really smiled. My life has become a series of awkward silences, of avoided glances, of a deep desire not to be seen. I've isolated myself from everyone, even myself.

The voices of my classmates, of my father, of anyone who has ever made fun of me, resonate in my head as if they were recorded. I hear their laughter, their biting comments, the insults disguised as "jokes." Each word is an echo that repeats itself endlessly, without pause.

My hands rest on my abdomen and the feeling of repulsion is immediate. Every time I touch my body, it's like I'm touching something foreign, something that shouldn't be a part of me. Sometimes, I spend hours in front of the mirror, looking at every part of me that they hate. My weight, my skin, every imperfection. I hate myself. I hate what I see. And that feeling... that feeling of wanting to tear myself away from my own skin won't leave me.

The door to my room opens, and my mother pokes her head in.

"Tyler, don't you want to have dinner?" she asks, her tone trying to sound friendly but coming across as hollow.

—I'm not hungry, Mom.

It's a lie. My stomach is growling, but the idea of eating, of feeling my body continue to grow, terrifies me. She sighs, but doesn't insist; she simply closes the door and leaves me alone, in the darkness of my room.

I think about how easy it would be to tell her how I feel, how alone I am. But what could I tell her that she doesn't already know? The truth is, I don't think she cares, not in the way I need her to. I feel like every single person who should be there for me has failed me. My parents, my "friends," even myself. We've all contributed to this hatred growing and taking root in every corner of my mind.

BETWEEN PROHIBITIONS AND BINGES

My father's voice still appears in my thoughts, his constant criticism. I remember how, as a child, I sought his approval in everything I did. Now, that need to be accepted by him has turned into a deep hatred towards myself.

I look at my hands, observing the red marks I have left on my skin from compulsive scratching. Sometimes, when anxiety consumes me, I squeeze my arms, as if that would help expel the pain or disgust I feel. But it does no good. The hate is still there, like a poison that seeps into every thought.

I try to take a deep breath, to calm down, but my mind won't let me off. All I hear is that voice, my own, repeating every insult that's been said to me.

"You're disgusting," I tell myself in a low voice, barely a whisper.

I look at the reflection in the mirror, at that face that grows stranger to me by the day. I no longer recognize the person I see. The boy who used to smile and try to be nice to everyone is gone, replaced by this empty, broken version who doesn't know who he is. I run my fingers over my face, feeling every pimple, every scar. I wonder if I'll ever be able to look at myself without feeling this repulsion, but I don't see how that's possible.

My hands clench into fists, and frustration turns into silent tears that begin to run down my cheeks.

"Why can't you be normal?" I ask my reflection, my voice breaking.

I remember the days when I tried to fit in, to be a part of something, to be liked by someone. But all of that now seems like an unattainable fantasy. At school, the cruel comments are constant, as if I were a reminder of everything that is wrong, a lesson in what not to be. And at home, my parents are unable to see the pain I carry, or perhaps they prefer to ignore it so they don't have to deal with it.

Sometimes I think about how easy it would be to disappear. I fantasize about a world where I simply don't exist, where I don't have to face this person in the mirror that I hate so much.

Suddenly, my phone vibrates on the bed. It's a text from one of my classmates, though I know it's not for anything good. It almost never is. I look at the screen, and sure enough, there's the message, a cruel joke disguised as an "innocent" comment:

"Hey, Tyler, have you ever tried stopping eating? Maybe that will solve two problems at once: you'll stop sweating like a pig and you'll lose that fat."

The screen blurs and my breathing becomes labored. I feel the heat of rage mixed with the cold of hopelessness. I want to respond, I want to scream at them to leave me alone, that they have no idea what it's like to live in my skin. But I don't do anything. I just put the phone down and sit back down in the dark.

It's at times like this that my self-hatred reaches its peak. Every insult, every taunt, it all piles up until I feel so small, so insignificant, that I don't understand why I'm still here. I get up and walk to the mirror again. I look at myself and silently let the tears fall.

"You're a failure, Tyler," I tell myself, my voice cracking. "You don't deserve anything, because everything you touch turns into something worse."

I don't know how long I spend like this, staring at myself and sinking deeper and deeper into this hatred that grows and consumes me. Finally, I let myself fall to the ground, exhausted, as if the entire weight of the contempt I feel for myself has drained the little energy I have left.

I close my eyes, and in that instant, I feel a deep desire for it all to end. For this life, this constant struggle to accept something that even I cannot see as acceptable, to simply disappear.

But when I open them again, I'm still here. I'm still Tyler, the same boy everyone despises, the same one who can't stand himself. With a shaky sigh, I get up and head to bed, letting myself fall into it, wishing that sleep would take me to a place where, for just a moment, I could stop feeling so much hate.

But I know that when I wake up, everything will be the same.

Chapter 7:

Every time I look in the mirror, I feel a mix of hopelessness and hatred. I don't know how or when this desire to change started exactly, but I know I have to. Maybe it's because I can't stand the idea of going to college being the same Tyler that everyone sees as a joke anymore. Or maybe I'm just tired of being the person I became after years of ridicule and rejection.

Today I turn eighteen, and at the end of the year I will graduate. That should be cause for celebration, but I can't help but feel a knot in my stomach. All these years, every one of my classmates, every insult, every laugh behind my back... it has all left an indelible mark. It has molded me into something I detest.

My mother knocks on the door.

—Tyler, happy birthday, honey. Are you coming down for breakfast?

—No, Mom. I'm not hungry.

I know it's a lie. My stomach has been growling for a while now, but the mere thought of eating anything else, of seeing my body gaining more weight, immediately makes me feel repulsed. I want to change. I want to be someone new, someone who doesn't carry around this skin that torments me. And I know that food has a lot to do with it.

Determined, I search my computer for information on how to lose weight quickly. I know nothing about diets or exercise, but I find hundreds of pages claiming to have the "perfect solution." Some recommend stopping eating certain foods, others suggest not eating after a certain time. I dive into a tangle of conflicting advice until I feel like I have a plan. A messy one, yes, but a plan.

Since that day, I start experimenting with giving up certain foods. Sometimes I skip breakfast, other times I decide to eat just one piece of fruit for dinner. I try to exercise in my room. Nobody knows about it, not my parents or anyone else, and I want to keep it that way. It's my secret. My mission.

Every morning I wake up before my parents and start doing push-ups, though I can barely manage a few before I'm out of breath. Sweat covers my forehead, and I remember the comments from my classmates. "You're a sweaty pig," they'd say. And every drop of sweat I feel reminds me of that. But instead of stopping me, it pushes me to do more, to push myself harder, to keep going even though every muscle in me feels sore.

One night, as I'm standing in the dining room pushing food from one side of my plate to the other, my father looks up and looks at me with an arched eyebrow.

"Aren't you going to eat?" he asks, almost as if he were mocking.

"I'm not hungry," I reply, forcing a smile.

He bursts out laughing.

—That would be a miracle. I thought you'd never get tired of eating like a pig.

My hands tense around my fork, but I force myself not to react. I focus on ignoring him. Just a few more months and I won't have to see him or my schoolmates. I just have to endure a little longer.

That same night, after dinner (or pretending to eat dinner), I go back to my room and look up more workout videos. There's one in particular, a guy who shows routines that promise "fast and extreme" results. I listen to him talk as he does an endless series of exercises, and something in his tone of voice convinces me that this is the way to achieve what I want. If I try hard enough, if I endure the pain, I could be a different person at the end of all this.

As the weeks go by, I feel like I've lost some weight. My pants seem a little looser, and I can do more reps of the exercises before I give out. Yet the mirror still shows that same Tyler I hate. Every day, I feel trapped in a cycle of effort that doesn't seem to yield real results. Desperation grows. I start cutting back more and more on what I eat, skipping meals, ignoring the hunger burning inside me. I tell myself that I don't need the food, that I just need to see a change.

One day, while I'm trying out a new routine in my room, I feel my legs shaking. Sweat mixes with the tears that begin to fall without me being able to control them. I can't take it anymore. I can't take this body anymore, this feeling of being insufficient. I let myself fall to the floor, exhausted, defeated.

The door swings open, and my mother looks at me from the threshold, surprised.

"What are you doing?" he asks, frowning.

—Exercise... I'm exercising, Mom —I reply, trying to sound normal.

—Why are you trying so hard? Since when do you care about this?

I want to tell him the truth, I want to scream at him that I'm sick of being the Tyler everyone despises. But instead I give him a quick, evasive answer.

—I want to look better... I want to be well.

She looks like she wants to say something, but she just nods, confused, and walks away. I'm left alone again, breathing hard, staring at the beads of sweat on the floor and hating every part of me that refuses to change as quickly as I'd like.

That night, as I lay down, I remember the way my classmates looked at me, the laughter, the mockery, the whispered comments they thought I wasn't listening to. The image of them, their mocking faces, is my motivation. I refuse to let them be right about me. I'm going to change, even if it costs me every ounce of energy and every moment of my life.

Days turn into weeks, and my "diet" and exercise become more and more extreme. It no longer matters if I feel hungry, or the fatigue burning through my muscles. The pain becomes a part of me, and I accept it as a necessary price to achieve the image I want to see in the mirror.

But a part of me realizes something is wrong. My mind feels increasingly cloudy, my thoughts slow and confused. But I keep going, because hatred for my body is the only thing keeping me going.

And so, every day, I say goodbye to a little more of myself, sacrificing everything to be someone I may never be able to reach.

Chapter 8:

I wake up and, almost without thinking, I grab my phone. The screen lights up and I go straight to social media. I've spent so many hours scrolling through images of perfect bodies that I don't need to search anymore; the algorithm knows me well. All I see are ripped abs, unmarked faces, perfect skin. Happy, confident people. People who seem to have it all. People who would never understand what it's like to live in skin you hate.

I scroll down and each image makes me feel worse. Here's a guy with a six-pack that looks sculpted, and I wonder if I'll ever even come close to that. Every like and admiring comment he receives feels like a reminder that I have never been, nor will I ever be, someone worthy of admiration. I dive deeper and deeper into these images, desperately searching for a way to transform myself into someone he doesn't despise.

As I continue scrolling, I come across a post from a model who is on a "liquid diet" and claims to have lost weight in a matter of weeks. In his caption, he talks about the "miracles" of his diet, how amazing he feels now. He wins me over with his perfect-toothed smile and that look that seems to say life is easy when you're thin.

Almost without thinking, I click on the link and read about the diet: only protein shakes, vegetable juices, and water. "Avoid carbs," "detoxify your body," "shed fat fast," the page says. I grab onto those words like a lifeline. I don't care if I have to starve or feel weak; if he did it, I can do it.

While eating breakfast that morning, my mother looks at me with some concern.

"Aren't you going to eat anything else?" he asks, noticing that I only have a glass of water and an apple in front of me.

—I'm not hungry, Mom —I lie.

30

BETWEEN PROHIBITIONS AND BINGES 31

She looks at me with a frown, but she doesn't insist. No one does. I feel like, deep down, no one is willing to see how far I'm sinking into this world of mirages of perfection. But I do see it, and I can't stop.

That same night, after skipping dinner, I turn to social media again. This time, I find an influencer talking about a "foolproof" workout routine. She's standing in front of a camera, smiling as she explains how this series of exercises keeps her in shape. Her body looks sculpted by fate itself, without an ounce of fat anywhere. She talks about doing hours of cardio every day and following extreme diets. Although she doesn't say how long it took her to get to that body, she convinces me that with enough effort, I could have it too.

I start following her routine that same night, and the fatigue is immediate. I can barely complete half of the exercises, and my legs feel like they're burning. My muscles are shaking, but instead of resting, I force myself to keep going.

—Come on, Tyler, you can do more —I tell myself, gritting my teeth.

I don't want to look weak, I don't want to fail. I close my eyes and breathe deeply, imagining that every drop of sweat is one step closer to that "perfect" body. But when I'm done, I feel completely exhausted. I barely have the strength to move. I drag myself to the bed and, while trying to catch my breath, I pick up the phone again.

I find more images, more people who claim to have the solution to my problems. "10 days to a new body," "extreme diet to eliminate fat in record time," and each promise convinces me that I am on the right path, even though I have no idea what I am doing. All I know is that if I follow their advice, one day I will be able to look in the mirror without feeling this hatred.

The next day, after skipping breakfast and doing a quick morning workout, I go back online looking for more answers. I find another model recommending appetite suppressant pills. He talks about how they have helped him control his cravings and stay fit. I stare at the bottle in the photo, wondering if they will work for me too. How dangerous can they be if he uses them and looks this good?

After doing some research, I find a way to buy them online. I feel like I'm doing something big, something that will ultimately lead me to who I want to be. But a part of me, deep down, knows this isn't right. That weak voice tells me I'm playing with fire, but I don't care. The idea of changing my body has become an obsession, and I'm willing to do whatever it takes to achieve it.

When the pills arrive, I quickly hide them in my room. No one must know, no one would understand. That night, I take the first one and feel a slight dizziness, but I ignore it. I tell myself that this is just the beginning, that this is the price I must pay. As the hunger fades, I look in the mirror and, for the first time in a long time, I feel in control. It is a fragile and dangerous control, but it is all I have.

Day after day, I stick to this routine of extreme diets, relentless exercise, and pills. My body is slowly beginning to change, but the cost is high. My hands are shaking, and hunger is a ghost that haunts me, even though I hardly feel the desire to eat anymore. I feel weak, as if my strength is abandoning me, but the thought of giving up is not in my mind.

One night, while scrolling through the web, I see another guy, with that same seemingly unattainable body. "Just try harder, Tyler. Just a little harder," I tell myself. Obsession has taken over my life, and I don't care about anything else anymore.

As I continue to look at those photos, I wonder if I will ever be as "perfect" as them. But deep down, I feel like that perfection is always just out of reach, like a shadow that recedes with every step I take.

However, I hold on to hope. Because if they did it, I can do it too, right?

Chapter 9:

The days have become a repeat of exhaustion and disappointment. Sometimes I wonder if I will always feel this way, trapped between the expectations of others and the hatred I feel for myself. When I look in the mirror, I see a stranger staring back at me from the reflection, a face I don't recognize and definitely don't want.

Today, as I was getting ready to leave for class, I stopped to look at my body in the mirror. My arms are slimmer, yes, but my stomach is still bulging, and the acne I thought had subsided seems to be getting worse. A twist of anxiety sits in my chest. I am not the guy everyone expected me to be. I wish I could feel satisfied with my progress, but every time I look at myself, I only see what I am missing.

"Why can't I be like them?" I whisper to myself, as my eyes fill with tears. I wipe my face quickly, not wanting anyone to see me like this. The last thing I need is more teasing or questions from my peers.

In the hallway at school, I pass a group of boys laughing. Without thinking, I look down and try to quicken my pace. "Look, there goes the fatty," one of them says, and a collective laugh follows. My cheeks burn with embarrassment. I don't know why I keep thinking that one day they'll stop doing this to me, that maybe one day they'll look at me like someone else, but that will never happen. I'm still the butt of their jokes, the kid who will never be good enough.

"Are you going to leave dressed like that again, Tyler? You obviously don't take care of yourself," says a familiar voice. It's Sarah, a once friendly classmate who has now joined in the laughter and mockery.

"I don't care," I reply, trying to sound nonchalant, although the lump in my throat tells me otherwise.

She laughs and gives me a look that says more than her words convey. I feel small, like I have no room in this world. This space that should be mine, that should be safe, becomes a trap.

During class, I can't concentrate. My classmates whisper behind my back, making comments in hushed tones that I can't help but hear. "Have you seen how he is? I don't know why he tries so hard, he'll never change." That phrase sticks in my mind, and the laughter resonates, echoing in an empty hallway.

The teacher tries to get my attention, but I'm too caught up in my thoughts. The expectations placed on me are so heavy. My parents expect me to be a good student, to work hard, and to graduate. But I just want to disappear. I don't want to be the "overweight kid" or the "ugly kid." I want to be anything but that.

As I leave class, I find my childhood friend, Ethan, waiting for me. He used to be my best friend, but now he doesn't seem to know how to act around me. His face lights up when he sees me, but then darkens when he notices I've sunk into silence.

—Tyler, is everything okay? —she asks, a tone of concern in her voice.

—Sure, I'm fine —I lie, forcing a smile.

He looks at me suspiciously, as if he doesn't believe my answer. I see the compassion on his face that hurts me more than any joke from my classmates. I don't want anyone to worry about me. "I don't need your pity," I think.

"You know I'm always here if you need to talk, right?" he adds, his sincere tone touching me, but also irritating me.

"I don't need help, Ethan. Just leave me alone," I reply, and the look of disappointment on his face makes me feel even more miserable.

I walk home, mired in despair. The pressure to be perfect crushes me every day, and I don't know how to break free. My parents expect me to get good grades, to continue with my college plans, but all I want to do is scream at them that I'm trapped in this battle against myself.

When I get home, my mother greets me with a smile, oblivious to the storm that consumes me inside.

BETWEEN PROHIBITIONS AND BINGES

"Tyler, how was your day?" he asks in that enthusiastic voice that used to cheer me up, but now only makes me feel more isolated.

"Okay, I guess," I reply as I walk past him and head to my room.

I close the door with a thud, and fall back onto the bed. The weight of disappointment is overwhelming. The image of perfection I've been chasing seems always just a step away, and I'm still here, stuck in this internal struggle that seems to have no end.

I scroll through my phone and see the posts of the people I follow, those sculpted bodies that seem to have life figured out. "All you have to do is work hard," they say. "Never give up." But what if hard work is never enough? What if I'm always the guy who gets left behind?

In a desperate impulse, I start writing a post on my social media. "I can't take it anymore. I'm tired of trying to be perfect when I'll never be." But before I send it, I stop my fingers. I don't want to be another burden, I don't want anyone to know how I really feel. So I delete the text and instead, I write something that sounds cheerful, something that hides the chaos in my mind.

When I look out the window, the sky is darkening, and I feel my world becoming more gloomy. In the distance, the trees are rustling in the wind, but inside me, it's all a tumult of emotions that I don't know how to handle.

Night falls, and with it, silence. In my room, the loneliness feels heavier. My thoughts become knives that tear at my self-esteem. "I will never be enough," I whisper in the darkness. "I will never be like them."

In the darkness, I realize that I have been seeking approval from others, while deep down, I despise myself. The expectation of others squeezes me, and my own internal hatred is like a chain that keeps me captive. I don't know how to break out of this cycle, and with each passing day I feel myself sinking a little deeper.

The tears begin to fall, silently, but I quickly stop them. "I can't cry, I can't show weakness," I tell myself. Yet it is a reflection of what I feel: an emotional chaos that I cannot control.

I look at the clock. The time is ticking, but the agony doesn't stop. Deep down, I know I need help, but my pride prevents me from asking for it. So I remain, trapped between the expectations I can't meet and the hatred that grows inside me, hoping that one day, maybe, I can find a way out of this labyrinth of pain.

Chapter 10:

The decision is made. After nights of contemplation and tears, I have come to the conclusion that I cannot continue like this. I must be thin. I must look good. I cannot bear the scornful looks of my peers any longer, the mocking laughter that seems to follow me wherever I go. If I need to sacrifice myself to achieve this, I will. I have been reading about diets, I have followed influencers on the networks that promise quick and amazing transformations. I have made a plan. This time it will be different.

The first few days are a game. I start each morning with a fruit smoothie and a small serving of oatmeal. Despite constant hunger, I feel hopeful. The mirror reflects back at me a reflection that is starting to look less grotesque. A pair of pants that used to be uncomfortable are starting to fall a little looser. My stomach, which has always been a source of shame, feels a little less prominent. Yet with each small step forward, the pressure grows. Every time my mother looks at me, I can feel that she expects something more from me. Expectations are like a lurking monster, and I know I can't fail.

"Tyler, you should try this!" my mother yells at me one day while she's in the kitchen. She's holding a bag of chips. She sounds amused, as if she has no idea of the torment that haunts me.

—No, thanks, Mom. I'm on a diet —I reply, trying to sound convincing.

—You're always on a diet, Tyler. Just try one. It won't hurt you, she insists, as she drops a few on the table.

"It's just a little," I think, but in my head, alarm bells are ringing. A little voice tells me that a bag of chips could ruin everything. So I stand firm.

Days go by, and the diet consumes me. Every meal becomes a mental battle, where victory is simply not giving in to cravings. But hunger is not an easy enemy. There are times when the emptiness in my stomach screams louder than my determination. Sometimes, as I watch others eat, a deep desire tangles in my chest, a longing I cannot satisfy.

One afternoon, the hell of my repressed desires finally catches up with me. After a tiring day, I come home and feel like I can't take it anymore. The pressure, the loneliness, the anguish of always feeling watched and disregarded, everything piles up in my mind. Without thinking, I rush into the kitchen. I open the refrigerator and start eating, as if each bite were a way to release all the pain I've been holding in.

First, there are some leftover cold pasta. "No problem, it's just carbs," I tell myself as I help myself to more. But that's not enough. Then I find the box of biscuits my mother bought. I pop them into my mouth without chewing, one after another. The sweet taste mixes with the salt of the tears that begin to fall without me noticing.

Before I know it, I've laid waste to everything in the kitchen. I start to feel dizzy, but the impulse doesn't stop. I feel both alive and dead, like I'm caught in a storm I can't control. Guilt and pleasure intertwine in a macabre dance as I realize what I'm doing.

When my parents return home, the chaos in the kitchen cannot go unnoticed. The table is covered in wrappers and leftover food, and before I can think of an excuse, I hear my father's voice echoing through the air.

"What the hell happened here?" he asks, his tone a mix of surprise and disappointment.

I feel my stomach churn. I can't look at his face, so I look away, waiting for the waters to calm down.

"I was... I was hungry," I manage to say, my voice shaking.

"Were you hungry? This is a binge!" he exclaims, taking a step towards me, his eyes full of mockery. I can't stand his gaze, that combination of disdain and criticism.

"It's not that bad," I try to defend myself, but I don't know why I do it. Embarrassment seeps into every word that comes out of my mouth.

—Of course it's serious, Tyler! You spend your life talking about losing weight and then you start eating like there's no tomorrow — his voice gets higher, and the pain stabs into my chest like a knife.

"I'm sorry, Dad," I murmur, feeling the guilt eating away at me.

"You're sorry? So what? Does that solve anything?" His sarcasm hurts me more than any physical blow.

I turn around and run to my room. I don't want to hear any more. I don't want to be a part of this horrible scene. I feel like a failure. In my mind, the voices of my classmates echo, the cruel comments they made to me at school. "The fat boy," "the ugly boy." Is this who I am? A boy incapable of controlling his own desires, of maintaining the discipline everyone expects of me.

I lock myself in my room and start crying. Reality feels too heavy. I don't know how to deal with this. "I want to be thin," I cry silently. "I want them to stop laughing at me." But the sadness and self-hatred are bigger than any desire for change. I feel trapped in a spiral that I can't break.

That night, guilt consumes me. I can't sleep, tossing and turning in bed, trying to find a way to escape this cycle. Images of perfect bodies I see online mix with my own reflection in the mirror. "You'll never be like them," I tell myself, and the echo of my own words feels like a punishment.

The next morning, I wake up with a queasy stomach. The binge has left me feeling empty and desperate. My parents no longer talk about what happened, but the tension in the house is palpable. Every look they throw my way is a silent accusation.

"Tyler, are you okay?" my mother asks when she sees me enter the kitchen, and her voice is soft, but all I see is concern on her face.

"Yeah, I'm fine," I reply, although the lump in my throat tells me otherwise.

I leave home with a mixture of emotions, a war raging inside me. The walk to school is a torment. I face my classmates, their stares, and

I feel the pressure is about to explode. But what hurts me the most is knowing that my own father, the man who should be my support, mocks me instead of understanding me.

I decide I must try again. After all, I can't afford to fall again. But the weight of expectations is overwhelming, and the internal struggle seems never-ending. I cling to the idea that change is possible, even though the cost seems ever higher. The question lingers in my mind: will I be able to find myself, or will I just get lost in this sea of expectations and hatred?

Chapter 11:

On the morning of my graduation, the sun shines as if celebrating with all of us, but for me, the light only highlights the darkness around me. The auditorium is filled with laughter and hugs, but I feel trapped in a dark corner of my mind. My classmates' smiles seem like mockery, reminding me of every moment of pain I've endured. The cap and gown are too big for me, not just physically, but emotionally as well. I feel like I'm drowning in my own skin.

During the ceremony, I try hard to smile, but it's difficult. My mind betrays me, taking me back to those days when I was the butt of their ridicule. I look out into the crowd, searching for someone who understands my struggle, but I only see faces that used to laugh at me. The feeling of being an outsider in a place that should be a place of celebration consumes me.

When the ceremony is finally over, everyone starts coming up to take pictures. My friends from school are elated, celebrating this achievement. They tell me to come, but in my mind, the voice screaming at me that I don't fit in gets louder.

"Tyler, come!" one of my teammates shouts, but I can't move. Anxiety grips me.

In a corner, I see a group of kids, the same ones who made my life miserable. They are holding a sign. At first, I don't understand what they are saying, but when they raise it, my heart stops. It's a photo of me, from when I was younger, with words written in big letters: "Fat," "Ugly," "You don't fit in here."

The air escapes from my lungs, and my body freezes. Hatred pours through my veins. The laughter that used to be distant echoes turns into deafening screams. My companions are laughing, and their laughter is like a knife that stabs into my chest.

"Look, the fatty graduated," one of them says, and the taunt feels like a direct hit.

"Tyler, this is for you!" another shouts, and the crowd laughs even more.

I feel like the world is falling apart around me. I can't stand this. My hands are shaking and heat is building up on my face. How can they still do this to me? Can't they just leave me alone, even today?

I turn and start running, away from the crowd, without looking back. In my mind, everything is chaos. Laughter echoes in my ears, and my heart pounds, as if trying to escape this reality. When I get home, the door slams shut. The calm of home seems mocking, as if the silence is laughing at me.

"What's wrong, Tyler?" my mother asks from the kitchen, her voice full of joy.

I can't answer. I can't speak. Instead, I lock myself in my room, the place that used to be my refuge, but now feels like a prison. Tears stream down my face and my chest feels heavy, as if all the pain of the years has piled up in a single instant.

The argument with my father is not long in coming. He enters my room, crossing his arms with an expression of concern and, at the same time, frustration.

"Tyler, what was that at graduation? Why did you run away?" she says, her tone stern.

—I don't know! Just leave me alone! —I scream, anger pouring out of me like a volcano about to explode. I've never shown them how I really feel. I've always tried to be the son they want, but I can't take it anymore.

"And you think that's acceptable behavior? You can't let what other people say affect you like that," he says, but his voice lacks compassion.

—You don't understand! You've never been in my place! —I reply, feeling helplessness consume me.

—You have to learn to deal with life. It won't always be easy —he tells me, and his voice is cold as ice.

BETWEEN PROHIBITIONS AND BINGES

"And what do you know about easy?" I retort, my words flowing like poison. The argument progresses, but every word he says hurts me more. At some point, I simply turn away, unable to bear his disappointment.

Finally, after the fight, I find myself alone. Loneliness envelops me and, for a moment, I can't take it anymore. The pressure feels unbearable. Without thinking about the consequences, I walk to the bathroom. I close the door with a thud. The mirror gives me a reflection that I hate. That image, that fat, sad boy who feels completely out of place, disgusts me.

Without thinking, I shove my fingers into my mouth. A desperate act that seems like the only way out of this sea of pain. Tears flow as I force myself to do it. Vomiting surges, and with it, a torrent of emotions. Every bite I've ever eaten, every moment of happiness I've tried to build, breaks down before me. It's like every piece of food is a reminder of what I'm not and what I'll never be.

I feel bad, but there is something liberating about it. The physical pain is mixed with guilt, and even though my mind screams that this is not the solution, I can't stop doing it. It's a secret I keep locked away, an act I don't want my parents to find out about, a dark relief in the midst of chaos.

When I finally emerge from the bathroom, I feel empty. Like I've expelled more than just food. Tears are still streaming down my cheeks, and the reflection staring back at me in the mirror is still the same. The same old Tyler, the one who feels insignificant, the one who can't quite fit in.

No one, not even my parents, has any idea what I'm going through. They think this day is a celebration, but for me, it's become a reminder of everything I've lost. Every laugh, every taunt, every image that's been thrown at me like a dart, has left a mark. And in the midst of it all, I realize that the real monster isn't just my peers, but the hatred I've cultivated within myself.

It's a secret I hold dear, a weight that suffocates me, and as I curl up in my bed, I wonder if there will ever be a happy ending to this story. But the answer is grim and dark, like the future that stretches out before me. The sun may be shining outside, but in my world, the darkness seems to have won.

Chapter 12

It's been months since that night. Since the reflection in the mirror became my worst enemy. And here I am, starting college, a new environment that should be exciting, full of new opportunities, but all I see is another prison where other people's eyes examine me, as if they know all my secrets. I can't stand the idea of being the same Tyler anymore, so I've started to change.

My parents think everything is fine. That the graduation "incident" is a thing of the past, something that is barely talked about at the dinner table, as if ignoring it will make it go away. Mom still asks if I want breakfast, even though she knows what my answer will be.

—Do you want something? I made you some eggs —she says, looking at me with a mixture of concern and affection.

—No, I'm fine, Mom. I woke up full, and I'm already late —I answer quickly, smiling at her so she doesn't get suspicious.

She nods, and her smile seems convinced, as if I don't need any more proof to confirm that I'm "fine." The truth is, my stomach is empty, but hunger has become my morning companion, a sort of constant reminder that I'm taking control. Every time my stomach twists, I feel a little stronger, like I'm in personal combat, and every time I ignore it, it's a small victory.

Lunch is the one meal I can't completely avoid. I'm in college, where the cafeteria is packed with students, and it's impossible for someone not to notice if I don't eat something. So I make an effort to eat the bare minimum so as not to arouse suspicion.

"Don't you eat too little?" asks Juan, a guy I usually have lunch with.

"I'm just not very hungry lately," I reply, shrugging.

"Well, just don't get sick or anything," he says, turning his attention back to his plate. I just nod, pretending to care.

My strategy is simple: I do enough so that no one cares or notices what is really going on. In the afternoons, after school, I go to English

45

classes with the excuse that I am busy. And in reality, I am busy, but not in the way my parents or friends think.

Back home, dinner is always a battle. Mom tries to put a plate full of food in front of me, but I give her a "I already ate with the kids" or "I'm not hungry, I had dinner late" that seems to be enough. My parents just nod and don't ask any more questions. Inside, I feel a deep relief and at the same time a pang of sadness. Every time I skip a meal, I feel a mix of satisfaction and emptiness, but the emptiness has become so familiar that it almost comforts me.

The first time I went an entire day without eating anything but that small lunch was tough. The hunger hurt, but not enough to make me give in. Instead, I began to see hunger as a sign of success. Every pang in my stomach is proof that I'm achieving my goal, that I'm finally gaining control. Because isn't that what I've always lacked? Control over myself, over what others see of me. Now, every time I skip a meal, I feel like I have power in my hands. I feel like I can finally shape myself, transform myself.

The nights become my most vulnerable time, when hunger reminds me that I am only human, that the body has its own limits. Sometimes my stomach hurts so much I think I'm going to give up, but then I look at the clock and tell myself that if I can just hold on a little longer, I'll be stronger tomorrow. Sometimes I walk through the dark kitchen, open the fridge and look at what's inside, but then slam it shut, knowing that by not giving in I'm gaining something that no one else understands.

My parents still don't notice. Dinner is getting shorter and shorter, just a few minutes of banal conversation. No one suspects that this is my new path, that I've started an extreme and dangerous diet. The idea of losing weight has become something bigger than a desire; it's almost an obsession, a goal that looms over me, day after day.

Some days I check my reflection in the mirror, looking for any signs, any changes in my appearance, but I still see nothing. My body is

BETWEEN PROHIBITIONS AND BINGES

still the same, an image I hate. But I promise myself that I won't give in. I need to see results, even if it takes time. Every day that passes, every meal avoided, is a promise that one day I will see the Tyler I want, the one people will respect, the one who won't be mocked or pitied.

On one occasion, my mother asked me:

—Are you okay, honey? You look different.

I felt my pulse quicken, but I responded with the same excuse as always.

—Yeah, Mom. It's just college, you know, it's a lot to adjust to.

She nodded, a flicker of doubt flashing across her face for a moment, but then she wiped it away with a knowing smile. No one wants to face what they don't want to see, and I'm an expert at hiding, at giving them the version of me they expect to see.

Every day is an effort to show the world a facade, but when I am alone, hunger reminds me that I am changing, that the sacrifice is worth it. I convince myself that this is the price I must pay. It doesn't matter if the nights are long, if hunger burns inside me, because I am on my way to what I always dreamed of. The comments of others, the mockery, the rejection, have become a distant echo. All that matters now is that one day not too far away I will look in the mirror and, at last, I will recognize someone strong, someone worthy.

Every step on this dark path feels like a victory. No one knows what I'm doing. No one notices the effort I put into avoiding every bite, controlling every impulse. It's my secret, my lonely struggle, and even though it hurts sometimes, I tell myself that one day this will all be worth it.

Chapter 13

The routine becomes clearer every day, more and more ordered. Hunger has become a constant shadow, a reminder that follows me wherever I go. And although sometimes I feel as if my stomach is an open wound that never stops hurting, I take comfort in thinking that this pain means that I am moving forward. That one day it will be worth it.

Today is one of those long days. I only had a couple of bites at lunch, just enough to avoid questions from my classmates. Now, in the extra English class, the hunger is so strong that at times I have trouble concentrating. But deep down, I feel fine, as if this pain is a sign that I am doing things correctly.

"Tyler, do you have the answer?" the professor asks, bringing me out of my reverie.

I look up and fake a smile, as if everything is fine.

"Uh... yeah, sure. It's..." I murmur, searching for the right words while ignoring the twist in my stomach. "The answer is 'always.'"

"Okay, I see you've been studying," he says, smiling approvingly. I just nod.

The truth is, I don't really care if he understands that I'm not at 100%. In this class, most students are here just to get extra points, and I'm no exception. I'm here to distract myself, to avoid going home and having to face dinner. It's easier this way, to stay here, feeling this pain that reminds me of my goal.

Next to me, Clara, a girl I met recently, looks at me with some curiosity.

"Aren't you hungry?" he asks me in a low voice as the teacher goes back to writing on the board.

"No, not really," I say, dismissing it. I lie so easily that sometimes I think I'm convincing myself.

BETWEEN PROHIBITIONS AND BINGES

She looks at me out of the corner of her eye, as if trying to see through my mask.

—You must be tired. You've had a long day —he comments.

"Yeah, I guess so," I say, trying not to show that I'm starving. I don't want to worry anyone or raise suspicions. I'd rather they think I'm fine, just another student with my mind on class.

The class continues, and so does the pain in my stomach. Every now and then I take a sip of water, feeling how the liquid momentarily soothes the sensation, but just a few seconds later, it comes back stronger. Still, I tell myself that this sacrifice is part of the process, a test I must overcome.

"Are you sure you don't want to eat something? I have a cookie here if you want it," Clara insists at the end of class, taking a cookie out of her bag and handing it to me.

I look at the cookie, small and seemingly harmless, but in my mind it becomes an enemy, a temptation that I must avoid at all costs.

—No, I'm really fine, I say, making an effort to smile at him.

She frowns, somewhat incredulous.

—It's just a cookie, Tyler. It's not going to kill you to eat one, he says in an amused tone.

My hands tense a little, and my smile becomes more forced.

—It's not that, Clara, it's just that... I'm not hungry, really —I insist.

"Whatever you say..." he replies, shrugging and putting the cookie away. I can see in his eyes that he thinks I'm being weird, but I try hard not to give him any more reasons to ask.

Finally, class ends, and I leave the room with an empty stomach and a mind full of conflicting thoughts. On one hand, I want to convince myself that I'm on the right path, that this sacrifice is temporary and that I'll soon start to see changes. On the other hand, a small part of me starts to wonder how long I can keep this up before the pain becomes unbearable.

I walk down the hall towards the exit and pass several students, some laughing, others eating. I wonder if they too feel trapped in their bodies, if they too are fighting the image in the mirror. But I know it is an unanswerable question. At least, for me.

When I reach the water fountain in the hallway, I take a few sips, feeling the liquid fill, even if only momentarily, that emptiness in my stomach. I imagine that every gulp of water is a victory, that every minute without eating is one step closer to my goal.

As I drink, someone taps me on the shoulder. I turn around and see Clara again.

—Tyler, I'm sorry if I was so insistent earlier, —he says, looking at me with a mix of concern and apology.

—Don't worry, really —I reply, trying to smile again—. I'm fine.

She nods, though she doesn't seem to entirely believe me.

—Just... make sure you take care of yourself, okay? —he tells me before giving my arm a little squeeze and walking away.

I watch her walk down the hall, her figure disappearing into the crowd of other students. For a moment, I wonder if anyone could really understand what I feel, this constant sense of inadequacy, this longing to be someone I'm not. But I quickly dismiss the thought. No one could understand.

I leave the building and start walking home, feeling the weight of the day weighing on me, and the pain in my stomach that has become almost a reminder of my purpose. Every step I take reminds me why I'm doing this. Because someday, I want to look in the mirror and see something that doesn't disgust me, someone who is worth it.

When I get home, Mom greets me with a smile and asks how class was. I reply without much detail, and when she mentions dinner, I give the same excuse as always.

—I'm not hungry, Mom. I ate something at the university.

She sighs and nods, not insisting further. Every time I avoid a meal, I feel like I'm winning this battle. Even if the price is the pain in my stomach and the worried look in Clara's eyes, I know that one day this will all make sense.

I go up to my room and close the door, letting myself fall into bed. My body is tired, but my mind is still active, projecting images of how I want to look, of how I would like the world to see me. And in those images, I am strong, I am attractive. I am someone that no one else could hurt or ignore.

For now, hunger is my only companion, and even though it hurts, I hold on to it like a talisman. Because as long as I can bear it, as long as I can resist, it means I'm moving forward.

Chapter 14

I wake up late again. My eyes feel heavy, as if the night hadn't been long enough to rest. But I did it on purpose, of course. Getting up late is the surest way to avoid breakfast and awkward questions.

I hear my parents' voices downstairs, and I close my eyes for a moment, seeking calm. I know that as soon as I get downstairs, the stares, the whispers, and the questions disguised as "concern" will begin. I take a breath, as if that would be enough to protect me from what is coming, and I descend the stairs, my shoulders tense and my feet heavy.

"Good morning, Tyler," my mother says as soon as she sees me. "Did you sleep well?"

"Yeah, everything's fine," I murmur, trying to sound casual.

My dad, sitting at the table with the newspaper in his hand, barely gives me a glance before making the comment I was expecting:

—Why don't you come down early like everyone else? It's almost noon, Tyler.

"I was just... sleepy," I reply, scratching the back of my neck, feeling like a kid caught doing something wrong.

He makes a noise under his breath, that kind of growl he always makes when something doesn't seem right. I want to say something, to confront him, but I decide it's not worth it. I know it will only make things worse.

My mother looks at me with a mixture of concern and disappointment.

—At least eat something now, Tyler. Look, I made you toast and there's some fruit...

—I'm not hungry, Mom. I'll just have some water and I'll be fine, thanks.

I try to smile, but she doesn't seem convinced. She sighs and nods, though, as if she knows that insisting won't change anything.

BETWEEN PROHIBITIONS AND BINGES 53

My father, on the other hand, does not miss the opportunity to launch one of his usual criticisms.

—Look, Tyler, if you're going to want to lose weight, skipping meals isn't the solution. Do you have any idea how unhealthy it is to do what you're doing?

I feel the color rising in my face and my throat closing up. But of course I don't stop there. There's always more to say.

—And that acne... —he continues, making a face of disgust as he observes me—. Maybe if you ate better, that would improve too.

It's like he's throwing one stone after another at me, like each word is a dagger that digs in a little deeper. I look at my hands, ashamed, trying not to let his words get past my skin. But they're inevitable.

"I'm... doing the best I can," I stammer, my voice barely a whisper.

"Really? Because it doesn't seem like it," she replies coldly. "At your age, you should know how to take care of yourself, Tyler. You can't keep making excuses."

My mother tries to intervene.

—David, that's enough. You know it's not easy for him. Sometimes he just needs...

"What do you need, Claudia?" he interrupts, raising his voice. "Do you want us to pamper him? Tell him it's okay? If we don't tell him the truth, who will?"

I look down, feeling my face getting wet. I don't want them to see me like this, vulnerable and weak. I don't want them to know how much each of their words hurts me, how each comment stays engraved in me, like a wound that doesn't heal.

"I'm going to my room," I murmur, turning my back on them and starting to walk towards the stairs.

—Sure, run away. You always do that, my father says, scornfully. —You can't face things, Tyler. Everything affects you, and you'll never get better like this.

Those words... those damn words hit me harder than I expected. Something inside me breaks, as if the fragile wall I had built to protect myself had crumbled all at once.

I stop at the stairs, and although I want to keep going up, I can't help but let out what I have inside.

—You know what? —My voice shakes, but I don't care—. You've never bothered to understand what I feel. All you do is... is... remind me how bad I am. I'm never enough for you, am I?

—Tyler... —my mother tries to calm me down, but I'm too broken to listen.

My father, on the other hand, looks at me with an annoyed expression.

—What do you expect? Life isn't easy, Tyler. People aren't going to sugarcoat things for you. You have to learn to accept reality and do something for yourself.

"Why can't you just... just leave me alone?" I scream, feeling the tears rolling down my cheeks. I feel small, insignificant, like every word I say is nothing more than an echo in the void.

My mother tries to reach out, but I back away. I don't want to be comforted. I don't want anyone to try to "fix" what I'm feeling, because I know that's not going to happen.

"Okay, do whatever you want, Tyler. If that's how you're going to learn," my father finally says, a tone of defeat in his voice.

Without looking at them, I run upstairs, slamming my bedroom door shut. I fall onto the bed, tears falling uncontrollably. I feel trapped in an endless cycle, where every day is a repeat of the last, where every word from my father becomes a wound I carry with shame and pain.

I try to breathe, to calm down, but every time I close my eyes, I see his face, I hear his voice, and the contempt in his words. I wish I was someone different, someone who didn't care, someone who didn't have to go through this. But I'm Tyler, the one who's never enough, the one who's always failing.

BETWEEN PROHIBITIONS AND BINGES

I spend the rest of the day in my room, not eating, not wanting to do anything but disappear. Food seems repulsive, like a reminder of everything that is wrong with me. My stomach growls, but I don't care. I'd rather be hungry than face another meal, another situation where I have to hear how much I disappoint my family.

At night, my mother tries to call me for dinner, but I don't answer. I pretend I'm asleep, that I don't hear her soft, worried voice. I don't want to see them again, I don't want to face another look of disappointment.

Finally, silence falls over the house. I stand in the darkness, feeling the hunger still there, constant and present. But I also feel something else: a kind of strange calm, as if this pain were the only certainty in my life.

And I realize that, in some ways, I've found my way to punish myself for not being enough, for not being the person my father wants me to be.

Chapter 15

I look at my reflection in the bathroom mirror, running my fingertips over my face. The pimples on my cheeks look redder than ever, and no matter how much I wash my face, they're still there, as if mocking me. I close my eyes, feeling a wave of frustration that makes my fists clench. I try, I really do, but there's no change, no improvement. Everything's the same.

The sound of my phone vibrating brings me out of my thoughts. It's a notification from a social media site, and when I open it, I see another post from one of those influencers with perfect skin. Her face shines, without a single blemish, as if the skin were made of porcelain. My gaze stays fixed on the image, and something in my chest stirs, a mix of envy and desperation.

"How can they look like that?" I murmur under my breath, not expecting an answer.

I look more closely at the post's description. She talks about her skincare routine, the products she uses, how she takes care of every detail. I don't think twice and take a screenshot. Then I start searching the internet for each of the products she mentions.

—If this works for him, it should work for me too, right? —I tell myself, as if this were the solution to all my problems.

For the next few hours, I read every page, every review, trying to understand which products are "good" for my skin. I come across terms like "salicylic acid," "retinol," and "niacinamide." I have no idea what they mean, but every site seems to rave about them. I buy one after another, as if the number of products I put in my cart is proportional to the chance that I will, one day, look like them.

Days later, a huge package arrives at home. I open it with trembling hands, carefully taking out each bottle, each tube, as if they were the holy grail. My mother passes by the door and watches me silently. Then, she can't help but ask:

BETWEEN PROHIBITIONS AND BINGES 57

—What's all that, Tyler?

I look at her, hesitating for a moment, but decide to be honest.

—It's... it's for my skin.

She stays silent, looking at the products and then at me. She doesn't say anything, just sighs and walks away. I don't need her to say anything; I already know what she's thinking. She thinks I'm overreacting, that it's not that big of a deal. But she doesn't understand what I feel every time I look in the mirror and all I see is someone who shouldn't be there.

Later that night, I lock myself in the bathroom. I arrange all the products in order, lined up in front of me, and I feel a little anxious but excited. This has to work, I think. This is my last hope. I look at the first bottle, one that says "cleanser," and apply it carefully, feeling a slight cooling on my skin.

—This is how it starts, right? —I say to myself quietly, trying to convince myself that I'm on the right path.

Moving on to the next step: a toner. I apply it with a cotton pad, following the instructions, as if each movement brings me a little closer to that perfect skin I so desire. As I go along, I feel a kind of relief, as if this routine is a form of control, something I can do to improve.

Days go by, and every night I repeat the process, step by step, like a ritual. There are times when I feel like my skin looks better, clearer, but then the spots come back, more irritated than before. I tell myself that it's normal, that it's just a matter of time, that this is part of the process.

One night, as I look in the mirror, I notice that my skin looks red, even a little swollen. I look closer and see small new breakouts. I feel a pang of frustration.

"Why isn't it working?" I ask my reflection.

My mother knocks softly on the door.

—Everything okay, Tyler? You've been in the bathroom for a long time.

I tense up, not wanting him to see my face in that state.

—Yes, Mom, I'll be right out —I reply, trying to sound normal.

I listen to him walk away, and when the silence returns, I stand there, staring at myself, wondering why I can't have the skin I want, why I can't be like them. I feel the tears building up in my eyes, and in a burst of desperation, I start touching each pimple, squeezing them, one after the other, as if that will make them go away once and for all.

The pain is sharp, but I don't care. I need them gone. I need to not see them anymore. I continue, pressing harder, until my skin is red and tender, and little dots of blood begin to appear. I stop only when my fingers hurt, when my face feels hot and my mind quiets, if only for an instant.

The next day, my mother notices the marks on my face.

—What happened to you, Tyler? —she asks, worried.

—Nothing, Mom. I got a pimple and... I was just trying to get rid of it —I lie, avoiding her gaze.

She doesn't seem convinced, but she doesn't insist. Sometimes I feel like she knows there's more behind my words, but she prefers not to ask. Maybe because she's afraid of the answer, or maybe because she doesn't know how to help me.

That night, I go back to my routine, applying each product more carefully, as if doing so will erase the pain of the day before. But it's getting harder to believe in the results. I look at my reflection and see only the scars, the damaged skin, like a mark of everything I am not.

"Why can't you be normal?" I whisper to myself, with deep hatred, without recognizing myself in the reflection.

Every day feels like a struggle. My hands shake as I apply the products, and my mind tells me that none of this will help, that I will always look like this. But I can't stop. This routine has become my only way of feeling in control, even though I know, deep down, that it's not enough.

BETWEEN PROHIBITIONS AND BINGES

I look at the bottles lined up, at the promises on their labels, and I feel a mix of hope and despair. What if I never get perfect skin? What if I always look like this, broken, imperfect?

I feel trapped in a cycle, unable to break this need to change, to transform myself into someone I'm not. And as I close my eyes, I imagine a version of myself, without spots, without marks, someone who looks good and is accepted. But when I open my eyes, I'm still the same.

Chapter 16

I lie down on the bed and stare at the ceiling, at the same spot as always. I don't want to think about what's happening, about how my stomach growls and reminds me of what I'm doing, what I've decided to do.

I try to distract myself, I open my phone and start scrolling through images of people with perfect bodies, perfect skin. I see how food doesn't seem like a concern to them; they just have control. Their lives look so ordered, so far from what I'm feeling right now.

I close my eyes and lie back on the bed, trying to block out the smell. But it's impossible. My mother must have made roast beef, with potatoes and something else. I imagine the plate on the table, the juice from the meat, the tempting aroma. It's so ridiculous that something like a plate of food has such power over me.

I cover my face with the pillow, trying to drown out the noises, to silence my mind and, above all, the hunger. But nothing works.

"Come on, Tyler. Hang in there. You don't have to give in now."

My own words feel empty and weak. I'm tired, not just of being hungry, but of this struggle that seems endless. I feel the tears building up in my eyes, the pressure in my chest that won't let up.

I hear my parents' footsteps in the hallway, and for a moment I feel like they're going to come into my room and ask me to have dinner with them. But they pass by. I've excused myself by saying that I have homework to finish, that I'd rather have dinner later, when I'm done. Of course it's not true, but they don't insist. They don't realize what's really going on, the struggle I have every time I sit down at the table. Maybe they don't want to realize.

As I writhe in bed, I feel my phone vibrate. It's a text from my mom.

Mom: There's dinner on the table, son. I'll leave it in the microwave if you want to heat it up later.

BETWEEN PROHIBITIONS AND BINGES

I read it over and over again, and each word is like a heavier weight on my chest. She thinks it's so simple, that you just heat up the food and eat it. But for me it's anything but simple.

I stand up and look at myself in the mirror. I see my haggard face, my skin red and irritated from the nights I try to "fix" it, my body that doesn't seem to improve, that doesn't transform. I don't even know if I've lost any pounds, but I still see that same person I hate, who doesn't seem to change. I move closer and see the pimples on my cheek, the dark circles under my eyes. How can I even think about eating when I'm so far from who I want to be?

My stomach growls again, loud and demanding, like it's screaming at me.

—Shut up! —I whisper, with a mixture of fury and desperation.

But of course, it's not that easy. My stomach hurts, I feel a pressure in my throat and my eyes burn. I start crying silently, without making any noise, trying to stifle the sound of my sobs with my hands over my mouth. I don't want them to hear me. I don't want them to know how weak I feel, how little I can control this.

—I just want to look good... I just want to feel good about myself, even if it's just for once... —I say between sobs, as if that would ease the pain in my chest.

I feel so lost, stuck in a cycle of hunger and despair. Every day is a struggle, and no matter how hard I try, nothing seems to work. No matter how many meals I skip, I don't see the changes I want. I feel like I'm incapable of doing this right, like I'm not strong enough to control my own body.

Suddenly, I hear my father talking in the kitchen. He's laughing, talking to my mother about something that happened at work. For a second, I feel a deep rage towards them, as if they are to blame for me feeling this way, for me being so weak. But I know it's not true, that this struggle is mine alone.

I take a deep breath, trying to calm myself, but every inhale brings back the smell of food. It's like torture. My mind screams at me to go downstairs and eat, to stop doing this to myself, that no one is forcing me to suffer this way. But then I think about how I would look afterward, about the hatred I feel towards my own reflection.

"No, Tyler, you can't give in. This is the only thing you have control over."

I feel the tears coming again. I hug my legs and rock back and forth in bed, trying to calm the hunger, the pain in my chest that is becoming unbearable. I turn my phone back on and scroll through the networks, seeing photos of people with sculpted bodies, of happy people, and I wonder if I will ever be able to look like them.

A voice in my head whispers to me that no, that I will always be like this, trapped in this body that I hate.

—I wish I could be someone else... I wish I could just disappear and not feel anything anymore.

The words come out of my mouth in a whisper, and I'm terrified to realize that I'm really sorry, that I wish I could escape this life, this body that gives me no respite.

I turn off the light and wrap myself in darkness, trying to make myself small in the bed, as if that would drown the pain that consumes me. Every time I close my eyes, I see images of the food on the table, of my parents eating dinner, and of that version of myself that I can never reach.

My eyes close, and the tears continue to fall, silent and constant. I lose myself in that emptiness, hoping that sleep will envelop me and, even if only for a few hours, free me from this nightmare that seems to have no end.

Chapter 17

I look at my reflection in the bathroom mirror, examining every inch of my face with an almost obsessive precision. My eyes pass over and over the areas where those pimples I hated so much used to be. Now, they are less red, less inflamed... some have even disappeared. But, for some reason, this does not give me peace. I do not see myself the way I want, I do not see that perfect face that I should have. There are still spots, imperfections that should not be there, that do not let me feel good.

—It's not enough... —I murmur, running my hand along my jaw and cheekbone, searching for any angle that will make me look better.

The silence of the bathroom makes my thoughts echo louder in my mind. The rage I feel grows, burning inside me like a flame I can't put out. No matter what I do, nothing seems to be enough to calm this hatred I feel towards my reflection.

I turn a little, lifting my arm and measuring the circumference of my wrist with my other hand. I wrap my fingers around my wrist, and this time, I can connect my thumb and index finger. It's thin, thinner than before, and I feel a pang of satisfaction mixed with something I can't quite place. Maybe it's pride, or maybe it's just confirmation that all this sacrifice hasn't been in vain.

But despite this, I feel a huge emptiness in my chest. Something I can't fill, something that seems to grow as I continue with this routine of not eating, of avoiding every bite.

My stomach growls, once again. It's a constant reminder of what I'm doing, that I'm subjecting myself to this hunger because I think it's the only way I'll find what I'm looking for. I swallow, trying to ignore it, but the discomfort in my abdomen forces me to put a hand on my stomach.

"You're not hungry, Tyler. It's just your body, not you. You can control it," I say quietly, as if with those words I can convince myself that it's true.

I remember the words I saw on one of those forums I follow, where everyone is obsessed with the idea of a "perfect" body. They said that true strength is resisting the temptation to eat, that the pain you feel is just proof that you are moving forward. I cling to that idea, even though hunger is driving me crazy.

My thoughts are interrupted by the sound of someone knocking on the bathroom door. It's my mother.

—Tyler? You okay, son? You've been there for a while.

—Yes, Mom, I'm fine. I was just... I was just washing my face, —I answer, trying to make my voice sound calm.

—Well, come down when you can. There's something to eat if you're hungry.

Hearing that word, "eat," makes my stomach turn in a strange, almost nauseating way. Like it's something forbidden, something I've decided doesn't deserve to be in my life. My mother doesn't understand what I'm doing, no one does. They just see food as something normal, something that should give me pleasure. But to me, every bite is a betrayal of everything I've worked for, all the pain I've endured.

—No, thanks, Mom. I don't think I'm hungry, I reply, although I feel a pang of hunger so intense that I have to close my eyes to keep from giving in.

My mother pauses on the other side of the door, as if hesitating to press on. Finally, I hear her footsteps receding, and her absence gives me a strange relief.

I look back at my wrist, wrapping my fingers around it again, making sure I can still close the circle. I feel a strange satisfaction in that, something that makes me feel like I have control, even if it's just for a few seconds. This is the only thing I have, the only thing that seems to make me feel better in this life that feels emptier every day.

But then, the hunger returns. It's like my stomach is angry with me, punishing me for denying it what it needs. The pressure is so strong that I feel a lump in my throat, and an inexplicable urge to cry takes hold of

BETWEEN PROHIBITIONS AND BINGES

me. But I won't give in, I can't give in. I've already come too far to turn back now.

I lean against the sink, breathing deeply, trying to calm the storm inside me. My hands are shaking, I don't know if from hunger or anxiety, or maybe both. This path I've chosen is exhausting, but I have no other choice. At least, that's what I tell myself.

—A little more, Tyler... just a little more and you'll be closer —I whisper to myself, trying to believe that these words will make a difference.

I look back at my reflection, my eyes glassy and exhausted. I have nothing that makes me feel good right now, except the idea that someday, maybe, this sacrifice will be worth it. Maybe someday, when I see the results, I'll be able to feel that all of this made sense.

With my shoulders hunched and my stomach still growling, I turn off the bathroom light and walk out, avoiding the gaze of my parents who are in the kitchen. I don't want to see them, I don't want to hear any questions. I quickly go up to my room, closing the door behind me. I lie down on the bed and close my eyes, hoping the hunger will fade, the emptiness in my chest will go away, if only for a moment.

But nothing changes. The hunger is still there, the pain is still there, and the dissatisfaction I feel with every part of myself seems to have no end.

Chapter 18

I look at my reflection, standing in front of the mirror in my room, my hands holding on to the edge of the furniture to keep from falling. I've lost weight, I can see it clearly. My cheeks no longer look round, my arms have less volume, and my pants no longer fit me. But even though I should feel better, there's something dark growing inside me, a voice that tells me it's still not enough.

—A little more... just a little more —I tell myself in a low voice, like a mantra, while my eyes scan every inch of my body in the mirror.

The past few days I've been eating only once a day, and each bite feels like a victory and a betrayal at the same time. My stomach rumbles constantly, begging me to give it something else, but I ignore it. I know this pain means I'm moving forward. It means the sacrifice is working.

Today, like every day, I got out of bed and felt the world shaking. As I stood up quickly, my vision blurred and I felt a throbbing in my head, as if my brain was protesting. But I just waited, breathing deeply until the sensation faded.

"Are you okay, Tyler?" my mother asks from the hallway when she sees me staggering a little as I leave my room.

—Yeah... I'm just a little dizzy, nothing serious —I answer, forcing a smile so as not to worry her.

She looks at me with a mixture of concern and distrust. I know she has noticed something has changed in me lately, but she doesn't know exactly what.

—Maybe you should eat something else, or at least have breakfast. It can't be good for you to skip so many meals —he tells me, with that voice that tries to be soft but that sounds invasive to me, as if he were questioning each of my decisions.

—I'm fine, Mom, really. It's just that... I'm not very hungry lately —I answer, looking away, because I feel like if I look into her eyes, she could see all the chaos inside me.

She sighs and walks away, giving up once again. I'm thankful she doesn't push me, because I don't know if I could keep my composure if she did. Part of me wants someone to stop me, someone to tell me what I'm doing is wrong, but at the same time... I want to keep going.

After my mother leaves, I go down to the kitchen and get a glass of water. I've gotten into the habit of drinking water whenever hunger becomes unbearable. It fills my stomach, tricking my body into thinking I've eaten something. As I drink, my hands shake slightly, and I feel a slight weakness in my legs.

—Just a little longer... I can take it —I murmur, as if just saying it out loud would give me the strength I need to keep going.

Throughout the day, every movement reminds me that I am weaker. Climbing stairs, lifting my backpack... even holding my phone for a long time tires me out. And yet, when I see my reflection in the mirror, I feel satisfied. I can see the change, and it gives me a sense of control I've never experienced before.

That night, I'm in my room, lying in bed, feeling the hunger consuming me. I close my eyes, hoping the discomfort will pass, but instead, my stomach continues to grow, begging for something. My head throbs, and a feeling of dizziness begins to grow more intense.

"Why do I have to be so weak?" I reproach myself in a low voice, hating myself for not being able to bear something as simple as hunger.

I feel a lump in my throat and, without wanting to, I start to cry. The tears fall silently, and even though I try to hold them back, I can't stop them from coming out. I don't know if I'm crying because I'm hungry, because I'm tired, or because I'm completely trapped in this obsession from which I don't know how to escape.

Suddenly, I hear a soft knock on the door. I quickly wipe away my tears and try to calm my breathing.

—Tyler? —it's my father, his voice firm—. Are you okay?

—Yes, yes... I'm fine, Dad. I'm just tired, that's all.

He remains silent, as if evaluating my words. Finally, he opens the door and enters, looking at me with an expression that mixes disapproval and something I can't quite place.

—Are you sure you're okay? You've been weird lately... quieter, more withdrawn. And... well, you're losing weight. What's going on?

—Nothing, Dad. I'm just... taking care of myself a little more, —I reply, trying to sound casual, but my words feel empty, like I don't even believe in them.

He sighs, shaking his head.

—Tyler, you take care of yourself by eating well, not skipping meals. You're playing with your health.

The words sink into me, but instead of feeling understood, I feel judged, as if what I'm doing is something silly, something insignificant.

"What do you care?" I reply, frustration spilling from my lips before I can stop it. "You've never cared how I feel or look, so why do you care now?"

—Because I'm your father, Tyler, and I don't want to see you destroy yourself —he replies, visibly upset—. What you're doing isn't healthy. You're skinny, you look exhausted... this isn't taking care of yourself, this is punishing yourself.

I stay silent, because deep down I know he's right. But admitting it out loud would be like accepting that everything I've been doing has been in vain, that all this pain is pointless.

—I just want to look good, Dad. I don't understand why it's so hard to understand.

He sighs again, shaking his head.

—Looking good doesn't mean starving yourself, Tyler.

He walks out of the room, leaving me alone once again, and his absence feels like confirmation that I'm alone on this path, that no one really understands what I'm going through.

I lie in bed, hunger still lingering, and close my eyes, wishing the pain would go away, for this whole struggle to end somehow. But deep down I know I can't stop, that this is the only path I know now.

Chapter 19

I woke up this morning feeling like the world was moving around me, like I was on a ship in a storm. Daylight streamed through the window, and I found myself staring at the ceiling for a few minutes, trying to remember if I had ever slept before. My body is tired; I feel like every cell is protesting, every muscle reminding me that I have no strength.

"It's just a phase," I repeat to myself as I get out of bed, although each movement is more difficult than the last.

My parents have been making a genuine effort lately. I've noticed them buying more fruits and vegetables, and trying to cook healthier meals, but all of this just makes my stomach turn. They don't understand what I'm doing. They don't know that I've cut back to one meal a day, because for me, every ounce I lose is a small triumph, one step closer to the perfect image I have in my mind.

"Tyler, are you ready?" my mother calls from the kitchen, her voice sounding distant, like it's coming from a world separate from mine.

"Yeah, I'm coming," I reply, trying to sound cheerful and normal. I don't want them to suspect that I feel like I'm about to faint.

When I get to the kitchen, I see that a colorful and healthy breakfast has been prepared. Fruit, yogurt, oatmeal... everything that should be good for me. But I don't care. The thought of eating makes me nauseous. I just want to get out of the house and feel in control of my life, even if that means ignoring what my body really needs.

"Would you like some oatmeal, honey?" my mother asks, smiling with that mix of hope and love that always makes me feel guilty.

—No, thanks. I'm fine —she fakes a smile—. I ate something before getting up.

My father's gaze is fixed on me, as if he's evaluating every word I say. His frown tells me he doesn't like what he's hearing.

—Tyler, you can't keep going like this. You need to eat, you really do —he says in a serious tone, but I only feel more helpless.

BETWEEN PROHIBITIONS AND BINGES

—I'm fine, really. I'm not dead. I'm just... not very hungry —I reply, while trying to avoid his gaze.

Deep down, what I really feel is that I don't want them to see how weak I am. Right now, the dizziness I feel is just a sign that I'm close to reaching my goal. Every time I look in the mirror and see a change, I feel like the sacrifice is worth it, even if it means feeling like a shadow of what I used to be.

After a while, my mother starts clearing the table and my father sits down, sighing heavily. The conversation turns to mundane things, but I can't concentrate. All I can think about is the pressure in my head and the weakness in my limbs. I feel like I could fall at any moment.

"Do you have classes today?" my mother asks, and I nod, even though I don't really know what classes I have.

"Yeah, I just have one math class," I say, trying to make it sound more interesting than it is.

I leave the kitchen feeling like I'm gasping for air. I need to get away, I need a breather. I can barely think about the math that awaits me at school when all I want is to find a place where I don't have to pretend I'm okay. But I can't give them the pleasure of seeing how I really am. Not after all the effort they're putting in.

Once on the bus to school, I try to focus on what I see around me. People are talking, laughing, but I can only hear a dull ringing in my ears. I feel my body swaying as I search for a seat. I hold on to the safety bar to keep from falling, but as we move forward, the feeling of dizziness intensifies.

At school, my classmates are in their usual routine: gossip, laughter, and disparaging remarks about those who haven't changed yet. I stand back, as always, finding myself alone, but at the moment it doesn't bother me. My mind is busy thinking about how I can continue to lose weight. In the meantime, I'm glad they don't see what I'm going through. It's like I have a secret that's mine and mine alone, a way to protect myself from the pain of their gazes.

As the day progresses, the hunger becomes unbearable, but I refuse to give in. I accept the pain, the nausea, because it means I'm on the right path. At lunch, I watch my classmates eat, energized and carefree. I feel isolated, but that's what I want, isn't it? I don't want to be like them. I don't want to be the kid who laughs and eats like he doesn't care.

In math class, I try hard to focus, but my mind wanders. The teacher explains a problem on the board, but the letters blur and the sound becomes a distant echo. I'm trapped in my own world, struggling not to pass out.

When the end of the day finally comes, my steps feel heavy. My whole body is screaming at me that I need to eat, that I need to rest, but I have to hold on. The image of myself as slim and healthy is the only thing that keeps me going.

When I get home, I feel exhausted. My parents are waiting for me in the living room, and when they see me come in, they are filled with concern.

"How was your day?" my mother asks, and I see love and anxiety mixed in her eyes.

—Normal, you know —I answer, trying to hide the fatigue in my voice.

"Did you eat anything?" my father insists, and I pause, feeling the weight of his question crushing me.

—No... I wasn't hungry. Seriously, I'm fine —he fakes a smile, although I feel the emptiness in my stomach growing.

My father frowns, but doesn't say anything else. Those words are enough to make me feel guilty, and deep down, I know I'm damaging my body in ways I shouldn't. But I can't stop. I can't give in. Not while there's still a way to go.

I close my bedroom door and fall onto my bed. I stare up at the ceiling and close my eyes, waiting for the dizziness to dissipate. The internal struggle grows more intense, and even though my body feels like it's on the verge of collapse, the voice screaming at me to keep going is louder than any physical pain.

—Just a little longer —I whisper to myself, as I let the loneliness envelop me.

Chapter 20

I stand in front of the mirror and feel a shadow looming over me. I pause, breathing deeply, trying to find something, even a tiny part of myself, that I can tolerate. But I can't. My eyes scan my face, searching for something I like, something that won't make me hate what I see.

"Why do you have to be like this?" I whisper, touching my nose, my forehead, every inch of skin I can find flawed.

My nose is what bothers me the most. It's too wide, too prominent. It's the first thing I see when I look at myself, and it's also what I see in every photo, in every reflection. Sometimes I think my nose is like a mark that tells the world that I'm not attractive. I've tried to look beyond it, to find some comfort in the details, but it's like every flaw reminds me of who I am and why I've never been looked at with admiration.

I remember all the times I was pointed out about my appearance. Casual comments, "jokes" that were said to be not serious, but that stuck with me. Words like "parrot nose" or "big forehead" still resonate in my mind. No one ever told me I was cute, no one ever looked at me as something special. No one. Instead, every time someone addressed me, it was to point out something I was already sick of hearing.

I close my eyes and take a breath. Maybe I'm being hard on myself, but I can't help it. This feeling grows, and the more I ignore it, the deeper it digs.

I hear a soft knock on the door and my mother's voice on the other side.

"Tyler, are you okay?" she asks, sounding worried, but I try to ignore her.

—Yes, Mom, everything is fine —I say quickly, without taking my eyes off myself in the mirror.

He falls silent, as if hesitant, but then he walks away, and I go back to my business. I look at my cheeks, my chin, my skin that doesn't have

74

the smooth, even tone I want. Nothing is right. I lean closer to the mirror, seeing every pore, every little pimple that seems to remind me that I don't yet have control over who I am.

My fingers slide down my face and I feel the tiny acne scars. They're there, reminding me of all the times I tried to "fix" myself. I tried to be better, I tried to look better. I've tried creams, treatments, I've even changed my diet to see if anything would change. But my skin is still not perfect, and every day that passes only reminds me of how far I am from the image I'd like to see reflected back to me.

"Why can't anyone see me any other way?" I whisper to myself, feeling the frustration building in my chest.

Minutes pass, and I'm still there, glued to the mirror. All I see are flaws. My nose that's too big, my skin full of marks, my eyebrows that aren't as defined as they should be. It all seems like some kind of sign that I'm not enough, that I never will be.

Suddenly, my father walks into my room without knocking. I look at him through the reflection in the mirror, and he frowns at what I'm doing.

"Are you looking at yourself like that again?" he says disdainfully, crossing his arms. "Stop wasting time and do something productive, will you?"

"Dad, I'm not wasting my time," I reply, even though I know he won't believe me. I don't even believe that excuse.

He snorts and moves closer, as if he needs to make his point clearer.

—You're obsessed, Tyler. You spend your time complaining about your appearance as if it's the only thing that matters in life. Don't you realize that no one is going to value someone who only cares about how they look?

—You just don't understand, Dad... —I murmur, trying to keep my voice from breaking.

—Understand what? That you think everything in life is about being pretty? Please. Look at yourself, you spend hours locked up here looking at yourself in the mirror, but that's not going to change anything.

His words hurt me, even though I was expecting something like this. His criticisms, his "advice" have always had this cold tone, as if there was never a space to truly understand me.

"I just... want to look better," I say quietly, trying not to sound so weak.

—It's not about looking better, Tyler. Maybe if you stopped focusing so much on the silly details and started worrying about the important things, you'd change something.

He doesn't look at me anymore and turns around to leave. I'm left alone again, and the echo of his words continues to resonate in the room. I feel like I'm on the edge of something, as if each word of his is a stone that weighs more on my chest. I look at the mirror again, this time with my vision clouded by the tears I'm trying to hold back.

"I don't want to be like this," I murmur under my breath, my words barely audible.

I want to change, I want to be someone different. But all I see is a mix of insecurities and scars. No one understands me. To them, it's all superficial. They think I care more about appearance than anything else, but they don't know what it's like to be trapped in a body you hate. They don't know what it's like to wake up every day and feel like you don't belong.

I sit on the edge of the bed, hands on my face, trying to erase the images of my own reflection. But desperation becomes a weight I can't lift. My fingers run over my nose again, feeling every little angle, every part I hate.

"Why can't I be different?" I ask the void, even though I know there will be no answer.

I'm tired of feeling this way, of this sense of inadequacy that seems to follow me wherever I go. For a second, I think about what it would

BETWEEN PROHIBITIONS AND BINGES

be like to not feel this weight, to not be looked at with so much hatred every day.

But that's just a dream. Because when I look up and see my reflection again, everything is the same. My nose, my skin, every imperfection is there to remind me that, in the end, I'm just a shadow of what I want to be.

So here I am, trapped in my own reflection, unable to escape this body that feels like a prison. It hurts more and more every day, and the worst thing is that I know that no one will be able to understand it.

Chapter 21

I'm alone in my room, the light off, watching my reflection fade into the darkness. I lift my shirt and run my hand over my stomach, feeling the skin, the fat that accumulates in the center and on the sides, as if they were living proof of everything I hate about myself. I clench my fingers, hard, wishing I could tear off every part that I feel doesn't belong here.

"Why can't you just disappear?" I murmur, not taking my eyes off my reflection.

Sometimes I think it's just a matter of time, that if I keep eating less and skipping meals, this weight I feel every day will eventually go away. But other days, like today, I feel a kind of desperation that won't leave me alone. There are still parts of me that remain the same, that seem to resist, and that fills me with frustration.

The sound of footsteps outside the door brings me out of my thoughts. My parents, probably, moving around in the kitchen. They've prepared dinner, and I know that at some point they'll come looking for me. They don't understand anything, they don't know that, for me, this food they prepare with such enthusiasm is just another reminder of what I have to avoid.

I sit in bed, hugging my stomach, listening to my mind fill with conflicting thoughts. Sometimes I want to scream at everyone, tell them how I feel, make them understand that every meal is a battle I fight silently. But then I remember how they react when I say anything related to my appearance. "You're overreacting," "It's just a teenage thing," or worse, "Why are you complaining so much?"

—Tyler, dinner is ready —my mother calls from outside.

I take a deep breath, trying to calm the lump in my throat. If I go out, if I sit with them and eat everything they made, I'll feel worse. But if I don't, they'll start asking, pushing. I slowly stand up and walk over to the door, pushing it open.

BETWEEN PROHIBITIONS AND BINGES

I walk down the stairs to find my parents already seated, serving themselves plates full of food. My mother smiles as she walks in and gestures for me to sit next to her.

"I made your favorite today, Tyler, isn't it great?" she says, placing a piece of cake on my plate.

I nod, trying to smile even though I know I'm not good at it. I feel my father's gaze on me, as if he's evaluating every gesture, every movement.

"Looks like you're eating less, son," he comments, without even looking at me.

—No, it's nothing, Dad. I just... I'm not very hungry lately.

—Well, you better eat well. Do you want to keep losing weight or what? —he says, laughing as if it were a joke.

I look down at my plate, at the cake waiting for me, and feel my stomach churn. Every bite I should be enjoying becomes something I dread, as if I know guilt, regret, will follow. I run my tongue across my lips, trying to find the words to respond.

"I'm just... trying to take better care of myself," I say, my voice low, hoping that will be enough to end the conversation.

But it's not enough. Nothing ever is.

—Take care of yourself? Since when do you need to take care of yourself so much? You have nothing to worry about. You're just a normal boy, stop thinking about nonsense — my father laughs, and my mother follows suit, as if it were the funniest thing in the world.

They don't understand, they never have. Every time I try to explain it to them, they end up with jokes or comments that seem to minimize everything I feel. No one sees that this obsession is not something I can turn off at any moment.

I lower my head and pick up the fork, taking a small bite into my mouth. The taste is sweet, I should like it, but all I can think about is how this piece of cake will turn into more fat stored in my stomach. I feel like I'm betraying myself, like all the effort of the past few days is going down the drain with every bite.

In the end, I barely eat half the cake before excusing myself.

—I'm full, I'm going to my room.

"So fast? You barely touched the cake," my mother says, a disappointed look on her face.

—I'm really full, —I lie, giving him a forced smile.

She nods, though I can see the confusion in her expression. It seems so easy, so simple to them. Eat, enjoy, live without worrying about what happens next. I climb the stairs again, returning to my sanctuary of solitude, and close the door behind me.

Once in my room, I sit on the bed, holding my stomach with both hands. Guilt washes over me, mixed with a hatred so intense that I have trouble breathing.

"Why can't you just stop eating?" I whisper to myself, my voice breaking. "Why can't you be in control?"

I remember the perfect faces I see on social media, bodies without a single flaw, without a single imperfection. People who seem to live without those worries, with the confidence of those who know they are attractive and desired. I just want some of that. A little of that peace, of that security.

But no. All I have is this distorted image of myself, this weight that never seems to be enough for others and at the same time is too much for me.

Tears begin to fall down my cheeks, and I realize I'm shaking. I clutch my stomach with both hands, willing the hatred to dissipate, for this feeling of inadequacy to go away. I lay back in bed, hugging myself, and feel the emptiness in my chest grow.

I'm caught in a fight that no one else seems to see, a game I lose every time I allow myself to feel a little pleasure, a little relief. And while my parents and everyone else go about their lives, laughing, enjoying themselves, I'm here, silent, bearing a burden that seems to crush me more and more every day.

—I can't go on like this... —I murmur, closing my eyes, trying to block out the pain that throbs in my chest.

But deep down, I know I will. Because even though it hurts, even though every day feels like an impossible test, I have no other choice.

Chapter 22

Today is one of those days when the house feels stifling. I need to get out, even though I have nowhere in particular to go. I put on a hoodie, something that covers most of my body, and step out into the fresh air. I close the door behind me and feel a momentary relief. I don't know exactly where I'm going, but I start walking, letting the sound of my own footsteps be the only thing that fills the silence.

After a while, I end up in a coffee shop. I go in and order the only thing I allow myself these days: a black coffee. The girl who serves me looks at me curiously as I prepare the coins and pay her. Her gaze makes me feel uncomfortable, as if she can see something in me that I don't want anyone to see.

—Here you go —he says to me with a smile.

"Thank you," I reply, without looking at her.

I sit in the corner, the warm mug in my hands, watching the steam slowly rise. I take a sip and let the bitterness fill my mouth, reminding me that I still have some control. It's not food, just liquid. Something that tricks my body and my mind, something that makes me feel like I'm filling a void, even though I know it's not enough.

When I finish my coffee, I leave the café and continue on my way, wandering aimlessly through the city. People pass by me, busy with their own affairs, unaware that there is someone among them who is barely holding on. I walk for hours, without stopping, as if I could leave behind every thought that torments me.

I finally reach a park. It's a quiet place, with empty benches and tall trees providing shade. I sit on one of the benches, arms crossed and head down. I let my thoughts flow without resistance, caught in an endless cycle of self-criticism and desire. I want to be someone different. I want to look different. But every day I feel like I'm failing, that no matter how hard I try, I'll never be enough.

BETWEEN PROHIBITIONS AND BINGES

As I'm lost in my thoughts, a sudden dizziness washes over me. Everything around me starts to spin, and I feel as if the ground beneath my feet is shifting. I try to take a breath, but it's like oxygen is avoiding me. My hands shake, and before I know it, my vision is blurry.

"Are you okay?" I hear a woman's voice, but it sounds distant, like she's somewhere else.

I blink and realize I'm on the ground. People have come closer, looking at me with concern, their faces full of questions. I feel the heat rise in my cheeks, embarrassed that I've drawn attention to myself like this.

"I'm... I'm fine," I murmur, trying to get up.

"You looked like you fainted, son. Are you sure you're okay?" a man asks, his voice full of concern.

I nod quickly, forcing a smile, even though my heart is pounding and my legs feel like they won't support me.

—Yes... thanks. Just... it was a bit dizzy, that's all.

I stand up, trying to look normal, but I feel my legs weakening. I look around, seeing the faces of those people who have stopped to help me, and I just want to disappear. I don't want their pity, I don't want them to see me as weak.

"You should get some rest," someone else says. "You don't look well."

"Thank you, really. I'm fine," I repeat, in a firmer tone, trying to sound convincing.

I turn and begin to walk quickly away from them. Every step is an effort, every breath reminds me that my body no longer has the strength it used to have. But I don't stop until the park is far away, until the sound of their voices has faded and only silence remains.

When I finally get home, I close the door behind me and lean against it, letting the apparent calm wash over me. All the pride I felt in walking away from those people dissipates, replaced by a consuming sense of emptiness. I drop to the floor, head in my hands.

"What are you doing, Tyler?" I whisper, my voice barely audible.

Every day is the same. I try so hard to change, to be better, but I always end up in this same place, feeling weak, broken. I remember the looks on those people's faces in the park, their faces full of worry, and I can't help but feel ashamed.

I stand up and walk to the bathroom. I look at my reflection in the mirror, but what I see doesn't comfort me. My eyes are sunken, my skin pale and lifeless. The body I see in front of me is not the one I want, not the one I should have. I run a hand over my face, wishing this was all just a bad dream.

"You have to do more, Tyler," I tell myself, looking into my own eyes, trying to convince myself that this isn't enough, that I can still achieve what I want if I just try a little harder.

I take a sip of water, just a sip, trying to calm the pain I feel in my stomach. It's a constant hunger, a need that never seems to go away, but one I've learned to ignore. I don't want to eat, I don't want to give in. If I do, I feel like I'm failing, like I'm betraying all the effort I've put in so far.

I walk over to my bed and flop down on it, staring at the ceiling. Everything in my life feels empty, meaningless, like every day is just a repeat of the last. Sometimes I wonder if I'll ever feel fulfilled, if I'll ever be able to look in the mirror and see more than just flaws.

—A little more, just a little more —I murmur, closing my eyes, trying to hold on to that small hope that, maybe, one day, all this effort will be worth it.

The room plunges into darkness, and in that silence, I realize I'm caught in a struggle that seems to have no end.

Chapter 23

—Wow, Tyler! How many pounds have you lost? —my aunt asks me, looking me up and down as if I were a prize won.

It's his way of saying he notices the change, of congratulating me, though it sounds as hollow as the echo that reverberates in my mind. We're at a family gathering, and everyone is around the table laughing, joking, while I'm barely holding on to a fake smile and an empty plate in front of me.

—I don't know, I haven't counted —I reply, shrugging.

My mother gives me a disapproving look from across the table, but remains silent. I know she is concerned about my appearance, but she prefers not to mention it here, where everyone seems to be proud of my "effort."

—Well, it's quite noticeable. You're a skinny guy! —my cousin says, laughing, patting me on the shoulder. —I should do the same. What's your secret?

A lump forms in my throat. My secret? I try hard to stay calm, to keep from breaking down in front of them. People keep talking, as if losing weight is the only goal in life, as if that's all anyone could ever want.

—Eat less, I guess —I say quietly.

My cousin nods with a smile, as if it really is that simple. Everyone seems to see it that way, as if it is as simple as following a "magic diet." But they don't know about the hours of hunger, the sleepless nights, the pain that accumulates in every corner of my body.

"Well, you did a good job," my mother says at last, trying to sound nonchalant, but I see the concern in her eyes.

I wish she would tell me something more, that someone would notice what's really going on, what I'm doing to myself. But she just smiles and changes the subject. And I'm left there, silent, feeling more alone than ever.

Later, I find myself in the kitchen, alone, looking for a glass of water to calm the hunger that is still there, persistent. The laughter and conversations of the others drift in from the living room, but I feel as far away from them as if they were in another world. I am alone, always alone in this process. I lean against the sink, letting the cold water soothe the burning in my throat a little.

Suddenly, I hear my mother come in. I didn't expect to meet her here, and for a second, I feel like I'm trapped, with no escape.

"Tyler, honey, have you eaten anything today?" she asks, trying to sound casual, but there's a tone of concern she can't hide.

I look at her, forcing a smile that I hope looks convincing.

—Yes, Mom. I've eaten, don't worry.

—It's just that... I didn't see you take anything at the table, and, well... everyone's talking about the weight, but... —he pauses, searching for the right words— I don't want you to take this too far.

Anger and sadness mix inside me. Sure, now he worries, now when everyone watches me and comments. But where was he before? Where was he when I needed someone to listen to me, to understand how I feel?

"I'm fine, Mom," I reply coldly. "I'm just... taking care of myself."

She nods, but I can see in her eyes that she isn't convinced. For a second, I feel like screaming, telling her that none of this makes me happy, that losing weight hasn't given me the satisfaction they think it has. But I keep quiet. There's nothing I can say that will change the situation. They wouldn't understand me.

—Well, if you need anything... —she starts to say, but I'm already on my way out, leaving her there, standing in the kitchen with her doubts.

The night progresses, and the house is falling silent as everyone goes to sleep. I stay in the living room, watching the television off, listening only to the sound of my breathing. My stomach growls, reminding me of what I have denied myself all day, but I ignore the hunger, as always.

At some point, I hear footsteps behind me and realize it's my father, who has just come down from his room.

"Can't you sleep?" he asks me, sitting down on the couch next to me.

—No. —I answer without looking at him.

He sighs, and for a moment we're both silent, trapped in a space that seems to stretch between us. Finally, he breaks the silence.

—Look, son, I know you're working on looking good, on getting better... but you don't have to take it that far. You're not... —he pauses, choosing his words carefully—. You're not looking healthy.

The anger I've been holding in all day suddenly comes out.

"Healthy?" I say bitterly. "Now you care? All my life I've been told that I need to change, that I need to lose weight, that my acne is disgusting... And now that I do it, you're worried that it's unhealthy?"

He opens his mouth to respond, but I don't let him. I need to say everything, even if he doesn't listen, even if tomorrow everything will be the same again.

"I don't know what you want from me," I continue, feeling my eyes fill with tears. "When I was fat, you made fun of me. Now that I'm losing weight, is that wrong too? It's never enough for you."

He falls silent, surprised by my reaction. Maybe he never thought his words would affect me so much, or maybe he just doesn't know how to respond. Finally, he stands up, uncomfortable, avoiding looking me in the eyes.

—Tyler, we're doing this because we love you... —he starts to say, but I can't hear him anymore.

—Then prove it —I murmur, almost without a voice.

He doesn't answer. After a moment, he turns around and walks up the stairs, leaving me alone in the dark living room. I don't know if he heard my last words, or if he just chose to ignore them. But it doesn't matter. I stand there, silent, feeling the loneliness and hopelessness envelop me.

Maybe this is the price I have to pay.

Chapter 24

"Tyler, can you come here for a moment?" my father's voice booms from the hallway, firm as ever.

I turn off my phone and take a deep breath before leaving my room. I find him in the living room, arms crossed, with a look I know all too well: that mix of disapproval and frustration that he seems to reserve especially for me.

"What's wrong?" I ask, trying to sound calm.

—Could you explain to me what you're doing to yourself? —he says bluntly.

I stay silent, because I know what's coming. He always finds something to criticize. And this time, I'm so exhausted that I don't want to argue, I just want him to leave me alone.

—Nothing, Dad. I'm just trying to take care of myself, —I finally answer, trying to avoid his gaze.

"Take care of yourself?" He laughs, but it's not a laugh of amusement; it's a laugh laden with contempt. "Tyler, have you seen how you look? You look sick. You're getting really old, can't you see that?"

The lump in my throat starts to get bigger. My chest feels tight, and I try to take deep breaths to calm myself, but his tone, his words... they make everything unbearable.

"You said yourself that I needed to lose weight," I reply, my voice shaking a little. "All my life I've been told that I should look better, and now that I do, that's wrong too?"

My father sighs and looks at me with a mixture of exasperation and something that looks like pity, although I don't recognize it. He comes closer and, without asking me, grabs my arm, as if he were going to inspect it.

"This isn't fitness, Tyler." He presses his fingers into my arm, wrapping them easily around it. "This is flab, all bone and skin. You don't have an ounce of muscle."

89

I feel my chest tighten with every word he says. It's like I'm tearing apart, piece by piece, everything I've accomplished so far.

"So what do you want me to do?" I say, my voice filled with suppressed rage. "If I stay fat, it's wrong. If I lose weight, it's wrong. No matter what I do, nothing is ever good enough for you."

—I'm not telling you to get fat, Tyler. I'm telling you to do it right. Look —he grabs my abdomen, with that hardness that makes me feel small, fragile—, there's nothing here. Do you know why? Because you're doing everything wrong.

I want to scream at him that he doesn't understand anything, that he has no idea how hard this has been, how much it costs me to get up every day, face my reflection, feel the hunger that eats me up inside and still keep going. But I know he won't listen. To him, this is just a matter of will, of doing the right thing, and he doesn't understand that I feel trapped in a fight I can't win.

"You don't know what I've been through to get here," I say quietly, more to myself than to him.

But he listens to him and his expression hardens.

—Past? Tyler, this is just the beginning. You look like you're going to pass out at any moment. What's the point of all this if you're destroying yourself in the end?

The words fall on me like a stone, and the weight of his gaze, of his judgment, becomes unbearable. I look into his eyes, searching for some sign of understanding, something that tells me that deep down he cares about more than just appearance. But all I see is disapproval, as always.

"Leave it alone, Dad," I murmur, pulling his hand away from my arm. "I don't need you to tell me what's wrong with me. I already know."

—Then do something to really change it, Tyler, he says, looking at me with a hardness that makes my hands tense.

I want to respond, I want to tell him that every day is a fight for me, that I'm doing everything I can, but the words just don't come out.

BETWEEN PROHIBITIONS AND BINGES

Instead, I just feel an emptiness in my stomach, a hopelessness that sinks deeper and deeper inside me.

He sighs, as if he's tired of me, of this situation.

—You know, I just want you to be strong. To be able to look in the mirror and be proud of yourself —he says at the end, as if that were the solution to everything.

—Proud? —My voice cracks a little—. I'll never be what you want me to be.

He doesn't answer me. He just stares at me, and in that moment, I feel any hope of him understanding me crumble. He takes a step back, turns around, and walks away, leaving me there, alone in the middle of the room.

I lock myself in my room and look at my arms, my abdomen. His words keep echoing in my mind: "flaccidity," "bone and skin," "no muscle." Before, I was only concerned about losing weight, but now... now I feel like it's not enough. No matter how much I lose, there will always be something wrong with me. My father has pointed out a new flaw, something I hadn't even noticed before. And now, that insecurity is sticking into me like a thorn.

I lie down on the bed, staring at the ceiling, and I feel the air getting heavy, everything around me starting to close in, trapping me in this frustration, in this hatred of my own body.

"Why can't I be normal?" I whisper into the air, even though I know there's no one to hear me.

I close my eyes, trying to calm myself, but my father's words keep hitting me, cutting me deep inside. Every time I breathe, I feel that pain in my chest, a pressure that seems to crush me from the inside.

Finally, I stand up and look at myself in the mirror, but this time I see nothing but the flaws he pointed out. My arms, my stomach, my face. Everything seems so... inadequate, so worthless.

I want to disappear, to escape from all of this, but there is nowhere to go, no way out of this prison I have built myself. I lie back down on the bed, letting the tears fall, silently, unseen. Because in the end, I know that no one would understand. No one would understand the weight of what I carry inside.

And so, alone in my room, I sink into the darkness of my thoughts, wishing I could be someone different.

Chapter 25

On Friday morning, I feel anxiety curling around my stomach. Today is the day. I stand in front of the scale I got at a cheap thrift store and take a deep breath. I've hidden it under my bed so no one can see it; neither my parents nor anyone else should know what I'm doing. This scale is mine alone.

Last night, I searched the internet for what a "healthy" weight is for someone of my age, height, and build. But those numbers don't interest me. I don't want to be in the "healthy" range. To me, that's just another word they've made up to make me feel like I can't go any lower. I want to be lighter, I want the number on this scale to be below normal. If I can achieve that, I'll know that everything I've done has been worth it.

I climb up slowly and look down, waiting with my heart racing. The number on the screen makes me feel a mix of relief and disappointment. I've gone down a bit, but it's not enough. I'm still far from the goal I've set for myself, far from that point where, according to my calculations, I'll look the way I want.

"Twenty pounds less and you'll be close," I whisper to myself, trying to find motivation. I close my eyes and imagine that day. The day when I'll look in the mirror and finally not be disgusted by what I see. I imagine everyone looking at me with a mix of admiration and awe. "Is that Tyler?" they'll ask. And in that moment, I'll know I've won.

I step off the scale and jot down the number in a small notebook that I also keep under my bed. Fridays will be my review days. My weekly ritual. Every Friday, this number has to go down. It has to. That's all that matters to me now.

At lunchtime, my mother watches me from across the table. I don't know if she's noticed anything, but lately her stares have become longer, more persistent.

"Tyler, do you want some more chicken?" she asks, holding the plate in front of me with a kind smile.

I shake my head. "No, thanks. I'm full."

She frowns, but doesn't say anything. I just push what's left on my plate, pretending to eat when, in reality, I'm just counting the minutes until I can get up from the table.

My father walks into the kitchen at that moment, and his gaze falls directly on me. I feel a chill run down my spine. He doesn't mince words.

"Tyler, you're eating like a bird. What is that?" she asks, in that reproachful tone she always uses.

—I'm not very hungry, Dad, —I reply, trying to sound casual.

—You say that every day. Look, kid, I understand that you want to look better, but that doesn't mean you're going to starve yourself.

My mother looks at him, uncomfortable, and tries to ease the conversation. "Leave it, honey. Tyler is in his process and..."

—Process of what? Of disappearing? —he says, letting out an ironic laugh—. Don't kid yourself, son. You don't have any muscle, you're just losing what little you have.

Every word of his cuts through me, but I try not to react. I just stare at him, silent, swallowing the answers I want to give him.

—I'm fine, Dad. There's no need to make a fuss about anything.

—Well, I don't see that you're okay. At the rate you're going, they're going to carry you out on a stretcher.

I get up from the table, not saying anything else. His voice becomes a distant echo as I walk away. I walk straight to my room, close the door and lie down on the bed, feeling a mix of anger and pain in my chest.

In the afternoon, I think about the scale again. The number I saw this morning is still hovering in my head, like an obsession I can't shake. I feel like every time I weigh myself, my life depends on that number, as if it's the only indication that I'm achieving something, even if it's small. I decide I won't wait until next Friday. I need to see progress faster. Every two or three days should be enough to notice it. And then I'll be able to monitor my progress better.

BETWEEN PROHIBITIONS AND BINGES

As I work out in my room, my father's words keep running through my head. "You have no muscle." "They're going to carry you on a stretcher." They feel like needles pricking my body with every repetition of sit-ups, with every push-up. He has no idea how hard I work, how much I sacrifice. He doesn't understand anything.

When I'm done, I lie on the floor, panting, and stare at the ceiling, feeling my muscles burning. This pain makes me feel like I'm at least doing something, that I'm closer to my goal.

At night, when the house is quiet and my parents have gone to sleep, I go back to the scale. I shouldn't, I know. But I feel that need, that urgency to know if there has been any change today, even if it is only a small one. I carefully step on it and hold my breath as the screen displays the number. It is the same as this morning, and my chest sinks.

"Why?" I whisper to myself, frustrated. "Why can't I see the changes?"

I climb back down and sit on the ground, disappointment falling over me like a shadow. Maybe I'm doing something wrong. Maybe I'm not trying hard enough. My head is a mess of conflicting thoughts and doubts.

I close my eyes, trying to calm myself. I think about next Friday, and the weight I want to see on the scale by then. I visualize a number, one that is below healthy, and I promise myself that I will reach it, no matter the cost.

—Next time it will be less. It has to be —I whisper to myself, like a kind of mantra.

But deep down, I feel tired, constantly hungry, cold in my bones. And even though I try to ignore it, I know I'm pushing myself to a limit that seems increasingly difficult to bear.

Still, I stand there, in the silence of my room, clinging to the promise that this effort will be worth it. Because if I stop trying, if I let the voices of others affect me, then all of this will have been in vain. And that is the one thing I cannot allow myself to do.

Chapter 26

I stand in front of the gym. I promised myself I would come today, but now that I am here, something inside me stirs with a mixture of fear and anxiety. My legs remain anchored to the sidewalk, as if an invisible weight were preventing me from taking the next step.

My hands are sweating. I can feel the gazes of those passing by, judging me. Everyone in this place looks like they were made for the gym. The bodies that walk through the glass doors look sculpted, defined, perfect. And I... I don't fit in here.

I imagine myself inside, surrounded by weight machines, men and women lifting more than I ever could. I imagine my muscles swollen, my arms full, my stomach swollen from all the weight. Just thinking about it makes me feel nauseous. I don't want to look like that. The idea of gaining mass scares me. If I gain weight, even muscle, everything will be ruined.

—Tyler, what are you doing here?

I look up and see Mark, a boy from my old school. The last thing I wanted was to run into someone I knew.

—Oh... uh... I just came to... —The words catch in my throat. I don't know how to explain what I'm doing here.

He smiles, as if he understands my nervousness. "Come on, man, you don't have to just stand there. It's not as intimidating as it looks. Come on, I'll walk with you."

Before I can say anything, Mark grabs my arm and drags me toward the entrance. My heart is beating so fast I feel like I'm going to faint. The smell of sweat, metal, and cleaner washes over me, and my stomach churns. I try to swallow, but my throat burns with anxiety.

Mark directs me to a corner filled with weight machines and dumbbells, as if he doesn't notice my discomfort.

BETWEEN PROHIBITIONS AND BINGES

"This is the place to work on your upper body. Do you have a routine in mind?" he asks me, as he prepares to do his first set of bench press.

I shake my head quickly. "No, I... I don't think I want to gain muscle," I mutter, feeling ridiculous for the way it sounds out loud.

Mark laughs, but not maliciously. "What? Muscle is what's going to make you look better! It burns fat and makes you look defined. Plus, with the weight you've lost, you need to gain some mass. You'll look great, I promise."

My mind is clouded. The word "mass" sounds like a sentence. The image of my arms filling with muscle, of my body gaining volume, scares me more than anything. I don't want to take up space. I don't want to be more. I want to be less.

—No... I don't want that —I repeat, more to myself than to him.

Mark looks at me, confused. "Tyler, you have to understand that gaining muscle doesn't mean getting fat. It's just improving your body. Look..." He raises his arms, flexing them, showing me the sculpted biceps. "This is all the result of months of work. None of it is fat."

I look away. I can't look at him without feeling sick to my stomach. What he calls "work" is, to me, the opposite of what I'm looking for.

"I don't think this is for me," I say quickly, trying to calm my rapid breathing. I turn to leave, but Mark stops me.

—Wait, wait, Tyler. Don't go. Listen, I know it's scary at first, but you don't have to start with weights. You can do cardio, maybe some light resistance. I promise you'll feel good afterward.

Fear and rejection boil inside me. I don't want anyone to see me here, I don't want them to think I'm trying to gain muscle. And most of all, I don't want to end up looking like them.

—No... I don't want to look big —I finally say, trying to make him understand something that I know doesn't make sense to him—. I don't want to win anything... I want to be... less. I don't know how to explain it.

For a moment, Mark looks at me as if trying to understand, but then shakes his head. "Tyler, you have to take care of your body. You can't just disappear, understand?"

I turn away from him and walk towards the exit, ignoring the way my heart is pounding so hard. I can barely breathe. His last sentence bounces around in my head: "You can't disappear." But that's what I want, isn't it? To become so small that I'm impossible to see.

At home, I close my bedroom door and take a deep breath. The sound of gym music is still in my ears, the smell of sweat on my clothes. I look at my reflection in the window and try to imagine myself there, lifting weights, trying to be "strong," as Mark would say. But all I see is the horror of filling out this body again.

I don't understand why anyone would want to do that. I don't understand how anyone could want to take up so much space. The mirror on my wall seems to mock me, reflecting every corner, every flaw, every part of me that I hate.

I bring my hands to my ribs, feeling them dig into my skin. This is what I want, I tell myself. Lightness. The freedom of not feeling imprisoned by my own body.

I lie in bed and close my eyes, trying to imagine what it would be like if I could really disappear.

Chapter 27

Today I feel more lost than ever. Sunlight streams in through the window, but even that can't cheer me up. On the table in front of me is a row of jars and tubes, a small arsenal of beauty products I bought online. They promised to work wonders, but here I am, sitting in the solitude of my room, feeling like none of them are going to work.

I look at the jar of facial serum I just bought, its bright label promising perfect skin in just a few weeks. "Miracle serum," it says. I can't help but think about how everything here, in my country, seems like a mockery of what I really need. Sometimes I wonder if all the money I spend on these products is worth it, but the hope of seeing a change always drives me to click "buy."

"What are you doing, Tyler?" My mother enters the room unannounced, and I quickly hide the jar behind my laptop.

—Nothing, just checking some things —I answer, trying to sound nonchalant.

She peers over my shoulder. "More beauty products?" she asks with a mix of curiosity and disapproval. Her gaze turns more serious. "Don't you have enough?"

I shrink back into my chair. "It's different, Mom. These are... they're special." Truth is, they're just my last hope for improving my skin. But I don't dare explain it to her. She has no interest in understanding how I feel trapped in my own body.

—Just make sure you don't spend all your money on that. —She turns and walks away, leaving me alone with my thoughts and my growing frustration.

Sometimes I feel like my mother doesn't realize how desperate I am to change. Not just for appearances, but for the need to feel good about myself. Every time I look in the mirror, what I see is a constant reminder that I am far from what I want to be.

I let my mind wander as I scan product labels, wishing I could afford those brands sold overseas. I've seen ads for them on social media, perfect bodies, glowing skin. Bodies that seem to tell me the secret is in what you apply.

"If only I could get my hands on those products," I whisper to myself, almost wishing someone would hear me.

Browsing online stores has become a daily ritual. I count every dollar I have and dream of what I could buy if only I could cross the ocean. But here in my small town, I only find limited options that never seem to work. When I use the products that are available here, they are like a constant mockery. They don't work as promised.

"Look at this, Tyler." I'm surprised when I find myself staring at my reflection in the mirror again. The imperfections seem to multiply by the second. "Who would want something like that?" I mutter under my breath, feeling each word stab me like a dagger in my chest.

The phone rings in my pocket, pulling me out of my thoughts. It's a message from a group of friends. Most of them are sharing photos from their latest trips abroad, including beauty products they're using. In each picture, smiling faces look at me with a confidence I can't match.

I would like to be a part of that. But I'm here, trapped in this room, in this body that I hate.

—I can't go on like this —I tell myself, frustrated. —This is no life.

I decide I have to do something about this. But what can I do? My mind is spinning in circles. I don't have the money for a trip to a place where I can get what I need, and even then, would it be enough?

Insecurity creeps in as I search through the computer for some brands that have caught my eye. I start typing names into the search engine, hoping to find a way to make this all work. But every time I do, a little internal reminder tells me that even if I manage to get my hands on the products, nothing will change.

"But what if they actually worked?" I say out loud, as I search for reviews online.

BETWEEN PROHIBITIONS AND BINGES   101

The reviews are overwhelmingly positive, and my heart is beating faster. What if this time is different? What if I can find a product that truly changes my life?

I can't help but feel excited. A surge of hope ignites within me, and before I know it, I'm adding more products to my shopping cart. However, in the back of my mind, a shadow of doubt looms. What if this is all just another failed attempt?

"Maybe I shouldn't..." I whisper, but I'm already committed. My hand moves almost on its own, and I finally hit the "buy" button. The confirmation appears on the screen, and though I feel relieved for a moment, I'm soon overcome with guilt.

"I can't go on like this," I repeat to myself, feeling tears begin to build up in my eyes. "I shouldn't need this to make me feel better."

My mind is spinning as I try to process what I just did. How much longer can I keep searching for perfection in a jar? The answer is always the same: until I'm satisfied. But deep down, I know that may never happen.

With a heavy heart, I put down my laptop and curl up in my bed. Anguish washes over me and I wonder if I will ever stop feeling this way. Images of those perfect bodies continue to haunt me as I find myself trapped in this cycle of desire and disappointment.

Chapter 28

Today is one of those days when loneliness feels heavier than the air I breathe. My parents are out shopping, and I'm at home, surrounded by the overwhelming silence that always feels more intense when I'm alone. The room is a mess, but I don't have the energy to tidy it up. All I can think about is how horrible I feel. Every time I look in the mirror, I see a stranger.

"Why can't I be like them?" I murmur as I run my hand over my face, feeling the skin, the imperfections, every bump and every mark.

My stomach growls with hunger, but fear hangs over me like a dark cloud. It's not normal hunger; it's the kind of hunger that feels like a shackle on my chest. I've been dealing with this constant pressure, a drive to control everything, and the thought of eating terrifies me. I feel trapped, in a cycle I can't escape.

Without thinking, I stand up and walk to the bathroom. The fluorescent light shines full in my face, making me feel even more exposed. I stare at my reflection, anger starting to bubble up inside me.

"You're a failure," I say to myself quietly. "Look at you. You haven't changed at all."

I close my eyes for a moment, feeling everything crumble around me. The temptation to vomit becomes a fixed idea, a plan that seems more and more attractive. Maybe this way I can get rid of this uncomfortable feeling that consumes me.

I decide that if I have to throw up, it might as well be now, when I'm alone. There's no one to see me, no one to judge me. I take a deep breath and lean over the toilet. With trembling fingers, I place my fingers at my throat. The sensation is strange, almost liberating.

"Just a little," I tell myself as I push my fingers inside.

The first time, nothing happens. Just a slight ickiness. But the second time, I feel everything starting to come out. The food I've barely eaten in the past few days mixes with the burning in my throat. I'm

BETWEEN PROHIBITIONS AND BINGES

surprised at how easy it is to do. The pressure that was weighing me down seems to fade away with each repetition.

—See? —she whispered to me—this is what you need to do. This way, you don't have to eat.

I continue, more and more eager to feel that relief. However, with each movement, the burning intensifies and my stomach begins to ache. As the action becomes more frenetic, I watch as the toilet water turns bright red.

"No..." My voice breaks as reality hits me hard. I stop dead in my tracks, my fingers still on my throat, horrified at what I've done.

Fear grips me as I stare at the stained water. The burning in my throat intensifies, and I feel weak, as if all the air has been sucked out of my lungs. I'm scared, really scared.

"This isn't right," I whisper to myself, trying to calm down. But I really don't know what to do.

I decide it's better not to eat than to throw up. The thought feels like a weight lifted from my shoulders, but fear and guilt set in immediately. My mind spins.

"What if I never eat again?" I mutter, the thought forming in my mind.

Outside, the sound of traffic continues on, oblivious to my inner torment. The feeling of isolation becomes more overwhelming, and I drag myself back to the sink. The burning persists, and I can't help but touch my throat with my hand. I feel a stab of pain, but still I tell myself that I have no choice but to go through with this new plan.

"Just this once," I murmur, pressing my lips together, feeling fear take over me.

I leave the bathroom and sit on the bed, feeling even more lost than before. Everything around me feels like a mockery of what should be. As I stare out the window, a flood of dark thoughts wash over me: loneliness, failure, the desire to fit into a world that seems so alien.

The front door opens and I hear my parents' voices coming into the house. My heart beats faster. I have to act normal, like nothing is wrong. I pull my shirt up to cover my stomach and try hard to put a smile on my face, even though my body feels so fragile.

"Hey, honey, we're back," my mom says, and the happiness in her voice feels like a weight on my chest.

"Hi," I reply, trying to sound nonchalant.

"How was your day?" my father asks, his eyes on the TV.

—Well, I just... did some homework. —I can't find the courage to tell them what really happened in the bathroom.

"That's good. You should eat something," my mother says. Her words are a mix of love and concern.

—I'm not hungry, thanks. —I say as I walk away to my room.

"Tyler, you have to eat something," she insists, her tone firm.

"I'm okay!" I shout before closing the door to my room. The echo of my own voice frightens me, and guilt immediately consumes me.

I sit up in bed, surrounded by silence again, but it feels heavier now. Tears well up in my eyes, and I cover my face with my hands, feeling all the pain I've been holding in come flooding back.

"I can't go on like this," I whisper, but I know I'm stuck in a cycle I can't break. My parents will never know what happened today, what I did. And I don't know if they'll ever be able to understand the pain I carry inside.

Chapter 29

There's nothing like the feeling of the world crashing down around you, especially when the source of that pressure is the people who are supposed to be supporting you. For weeks now, I've been feeling like a clown in a sideshow, trying to please everyone while simultaneously feeling trapped in my own expectations. The image I have in my mind of what I should be has taken more of a toll on me than I can bear.

Today, after receiving a package she had been eagerly awaiting, my mother decided to make her famous grand entrance. The front door of the house opened with a familiar creak, and suddenly, her voice rang out like thunder in the quiet of the afternoon.

"Tyler?" she calls out, and my heart races at the sound of her name.

From my room, I force a smile, though I know it's a forced one. All I can think about is the new cleansing gel that finally arrived, a product that promised me the best skin ever. My hands are eager to try it, but I know my mother's arrival will bring trouble.

—Where are you? —he asks as he climbs the stairs.

—In my room —I answer, trying to sound nonchalant.

The door swings open and there she is, with her expression of disbelief.

"What is this?" he says, pointing to the open box on my desk.

"It's just... beauty products I ordered," I say, feeling the discomfort growing in my chest.

"More beauty products? How much did you spend this time?" Her tone turns sharp, and I can feel the tension in the air.

—It's not that much, Mom. —I try to play it down. —It's just things I need.

She comes closer, holding up the cleansing gel as if it were evidence against me.

—Do you need it? Really? Because it seems like you're spending money on this instead of things that really matter, like your food.

"It's not that simple," I say, trying to remain calm. "It makes me feel better."

"Better?" His laugh is bitter. "You look the same as always. Why can't you accept that maybe you don't need all these products?"

The words are like knives, each one cutting a little deeper. I know he says it out of concern, but there's also a trace of contempt that I can't ignore.

—You don't understand. —My voice shakes a little—. I'm trying to get better. I want to look good.

"What does that mean?" he interrupts, folding his arms. "Spending money you should be using for food on creams and potions that probably don't work?"

"You're exaggerating, Mom," I reply, clenching my fists. "I don't have to explain how I spend my money."

She sighs, her expression a mixture of frustration and sadness.

—You're not okay, Tyler. You're looking thinner and thinner. You can't keep going like this. Your health is the most important thing.

—I know you mean it because you care, but... —my voice breaks— I'm trying to do the best I can.

—The best thing you can do is eat enough and not spend money on superficial things. You have to start being more responsible.

His words resonate in my head like an echo that never stops. I feel smaller and smaller, more and more powerless.

"What if I can't?" I ask, desperation lacing my voice. "What if I'm never satisfied with how I look?"

—That's crazy, Tyler. You have to learn to accept yourself as you are. —His tone softens a little, but the reality of his words hurts me just the same.

"So what if I can't?" I repeat, my voice rising in volume. "There's no way I can feel okay if I keep looking like this."

She looks at me, her eyes filled with a mix of compassion and frustration.

BETWEEN PROHIBITIONS AND BINGES 107

"How? This thin?" His voice is a whisper, but each word is like a gunshot. "This isn't healthy."

I take a step back, feeling cornered. The walls of my room seem to close in, and I suddenly feel trapped in a space I once considered safe.

"I don't want to talk about this anymore," I say, trying to control my voice so it doesn't shake.

—I'm not going to let this go, Tyler. This is serious. —She crosses her arms, standing her ground. —You need help.

My eyes fill with tears, and I turn away to avoid being seen like this. Pride gets in my way, but vulnerability screams inside me too.

"I don't need help," I repeat, even though I know it's a lie.

—You know you need her. And I can't just stand by and watch you fall apart. —My mother's voice is like a rock in my chest, heavy and painful.

I don't know what else to say, so I stay quiet, feeling even more isolated. Every word we exchange feels like another brick in the wall I'm building around myself.

"Tyler, please," she insists, her tone softer now. "I just want you to be happy."

"You can't tell me what will make me happy," my voice cracks, and I realize I've raised my voice. "No one knows what I'm going through."

She falls silent, and for a moment, time seems to stop.

—What do you mean? —he asks cautiously.

"You don't understand what it's like." Sighing, I flop down onto the bed. "Nothing I do is ever good enough. Every time I try to improve, I feel like I'm failing."

"You're not failing." His voice is soft, but his gaze is intense. "You're just in a dark place. We've all been there."

—No, not everyone. —I answer bitterly. —You don't understand. Nobody understands.

—So help me understand. I'm here for you, but you have to let me in. —She approaches me, her expression serious and worried.

But I feel so trapped, so lost in this sea of insecurities and criticism that I can't see a way out. Anger starts bubbling up again, and I stand up abruptly.

"Do you want me to help you understand?" My voice becomes sharp. "Do you want to know how I feel? Do you want to know how it is that, even when I look in the mirror, I can't stand what I see?"

She falls silent, and the air between us feels thick. I don't really know if I want her to understand. Maybe she just wants me to be left alone in my misery, in my struggle.

"I love you, Tyler. I want you to feel good about yourself." His tone is soft, almost like a plea, but I'm too blinded by pain to accept it.

"I want to get out of here," I say, and as I do, I realize that tears are welling up in my eyes, taking all my pride with them.

I run out of my room, the sound of his voice behind me, but I can't stay and listen any longer. I don't want to know that he's trying to help me. I don't know if I can handle being told that everything will be okay when I feel so lost.

—Tyler, come back here! —she yells, but I'm outside the house, the cold air hitting my face, and all I can think about is the pain I'm in.

As I walk away, an empty feeling settles in my chest. I've reached a point where my family's criticism feels like a prison, and I realize there's no way to escape it. There's no way to escape myself.

Chapter 30

I left the house without looking back, as if the fresh air outside could wash away the anguish inside me. My mother's words kept echoing in my mind: "Tyler, this isn't healthy." The truth is, I had no idea what healthy was. All I knew was that everything in my life seemed to be spiraling out of control, and every time I tried to put it in order, something fell apart.

I walked to the park, each step echoing my loneliness. The sky was clear, but my thoughts were a storm. I plopped down on an empty bench, watching the people passing by. I saw a girl approaching. She was thin, almost ethereal, as if she could vanish into thin air. We looked at each other briefly, and in that instant I felt a connection that made me shudder. She seemed to carry her own weight, too, even though no one could see it.

"Do you know what this is?" I asked myself as I watched her walk away. That shared look, however fleeting, was a reflection of what we all felt, an unspoken understanding that bound us together on this dark journey. But I also realized that, despite what we might share, our company would only lead us closer to destruction. What happened when two lost souls found each other? Instead of helping, perhaps they only pushed each other further into the abyss.

With that thought in mind, I got up from the bench and decided to head back home. The walk back felt longer than it should have, as if the weight of my thoughts had become heavier. My parents were waiting for me, and I knew the argument wasn't over yet.

When I opened the door, the atmosphere was tense. My mother was in the kitchen, and I could sense her concern even before I saw her. My father was in the living room, and his gaze was like lightning, sharp and direct.

"Where have you been?" my mother asked in a low but firm voice.

"I just went for a walk," I said, trying to make my tone sound nonchalant, but I couldn't stop the shaking in my hands from giving away.

"A walk, huh? A walk to escape reality?" my father entered the conversation, his voice laced with disdain. "You're not solving anything, Tyler."

—I'm not running away from anything. I just need time to think —I replied, trying to remain calm.

"You always have an excuse," my mother said, coming closer. "Is it too much to ask that you take care of yourself?"

The conversation became a vicious circle, and my words began to come out in fits and starts. Frustration and anger flooded through me.

"I don't understand why you can't just leave me alone!" I shouted, and at that moment, I felt the pressure boiling over. "I'm not a child. I know what I'm doing."

My father approached, his expression one of suppressed rage.

"Do you know what you're doing, Tyler? You're destroying your life. You don't look good, and you're not okay." His tone became more menacing. "You can't keep going like this."

"What do you know about what it means to be okay?" I challenged, feeling like every word was a nail in the coffin of my patience. "You don't know what I'm going through."

"And you think you do know that?" my father replied, moving even closer. "You're just a child who refuses to accept reality."

I felt the heat of anger consume me, and my body tensed. I wanted to scream, I wanted to make them understand, but instead my words turned to thunderous silence.

—Just... —I started to say, but my voice broke.

"Just what?" my father asked, his mocking tone turning into a sword. "Are you going to keep lying to us?"

BETWEEN PROHIBITIONS AND BINGES

A chill ran down my spine. My mother was about to intervene, but she could no longer bear it. On impulse, I raised my hand and shouted to my father:

—Enough! I can't take it anymore!

That's when everything turned into a whirlwind. My father, in a moment of anger, pushed me and hit me. The pain surprised me, but what hurt me more was the betrayal I felt. I didn't expect that from him.

I fell to the ground, stunned, and as I recovered, I saw the horror in my mother's eyes. She came closer, trying to intervene, but her look was one of helplessness.

—What have you done?! —she screamed.

"He asked for it!" my father replied, his voice full of rage. "He's not going to keep coming up with his excuses and his nonsense."

I slowly stood up, and although the pain on my face was intense, the pain in my chest was even more unbearable. I didn't want my mother to see me like this, I didn't want anyone to.

Without saying a word, I turned around and headed to my room, feeling the weight of the world fall on my shoulders. The door closed behind me with a thud, and in that moment, I felt like I was swallowed by emptiness.

I fell back onto the bed, and the tears began to flow. I didn't understand how it had come to this, how the arguments, criticisms, and expectations had turned into such a fierce struggle.

I didn't know if I could bear this. I knew there was something inside me that was breaking, something that couldn't be fixed with words. I was stuck in a cycle of pain and restlessness, and as much as I wanted to be understood, I knew that at the end of the day, it was only me who could fight my demons.

I cried from the pain, from the loneliness, from the inability to make myself understood. The voices in my head became louder, heavier. It was an echo of what I couldn't escape.

And as silence settled in my room, I realized that the real battle was not just against my body, but also against the perception of others, against expectations that no one but me had created. I knew I had to find a way out of this darkness, but I didn't know how. I could only keep going, fighting this internal war that consumed me.

Chapter 31

The days passed with the monotony of a clock without hands, and every time the sunlight filtered through the cracks in my room, I wondered if I really wanted to face the world outside. The distance that had been created between my parents and me was palpable, almost like a wall that had been raised between us, and every attempt to communicate felt like a failed attempt to tear it down.

It was a morning like any other. I lay in my bed, staring at the ceiling, feeling the sadness creep over me again. It had been so long since we shared a meal or a meaningful conversation. The last time we met for dinner, my father looked at me as if he was about to say something, but the words never came. Instead, he got up from the table and walked away, leaving behind a silence that echoed louder than any argument we had ever had.

I decided there was nothing to be done, so I got dressed and went down to the living room. My mother was in the kitchen, but I didn't see her. I could only hear the sound of running water and dishes being moved. I decided it was best to avoid her. The echo of the friction between us still hurt, and I didn't know how to handle it.

I grabbed my phone and decided to go out for a walk. The fresh air would help clear my mind. As I walked through the neighborhood, the streets seemed emptier than usual. The families that usually strolled together were gone, and all that remained were familiar faces waving hello without asking questions, as if they knew there were no answers to give.

When I got home, the tension was even stronger. My father was in the living room watching television. He didn't look at me. I felt a knot in my stomach.

"Hi," I said, trying to break the ice, but my voice felt small in the room.

"Hello," he replied, without taking his eyes off the screen. His tone was as cold as the air coming through the open window.

I decided it wasn't worth it to insist. I went to my room and sat on the bed, feeling so isolated that even the walls seemed to close in on me. My mother came in shortly after, her eyes fixed on her phone.

"Tyler, aren't you going to lunch?" she asked, as if it were a mere formality.

"I'm not hungry," I replied, sensing that the truth was much more complicated than that.

"Well, I just wanted to know," he said, his tone lacking the concern it usually had. It was just a routine check to make sure he was still alive.

The lack of connection hit home. Family lunches had become a forgotten tradition. Before, it was a time when we shared stories, laughter, and sometimes even tears. But now, everyone seemed more interested in the outside world than in what was happening under the same roof.

As I was thinking about all this, my parents started yelling in the kitchen. I stood up, feeling the need to know what was going on, but I stood in the hallway, listening to snatches of the conversation.

"I can't ignore this any longer. Tyler needs help," my mother said, her voice filled with concern.

—Help? He doesn't want help! He's just in his own world and doesn't want to listen to anyone — my father replied in frustration.

"It's not about wanting or not wanting. It's about taking care of our son. Something's not right, and we know it," she replied, her tone raised.

The mention of "help" rang like a bell for me. I had never seen my situation from that perspective. In my mind, it was just a matter of willpower; I could change it, I could do it alone. But hearing my parents talk about it filled me with panic.

I decided it was best to go back to my room, and so I did. I closed the door and fell back onto the bed, feeling the pressure in my chest

BETWEEN PROHIBITIONS AND BINGES
115

increase. The thought of them thinking I needed help made me feel vulnerable.

The nights became a sea of loneliness. Often, I didn't hear a single sound in the house. There were no more after-dinner conversations, no weekend plans. Everyone seemed to be lost in their own world, and the connection we once had was fading like a mirage.

One day, while I was sitting in the kitchen, I heard my mother talking on the phone. The conversation turned serious.

—Yes, I think we should consider an intervention. I don't know how much longer I can stand to see Tyler like this... —her voice cracked a little.

My heart sank. I didn't want my mother to feel this way, but I couldn't help but feel like a failure. The fact that she felt like I needed to do something, that she wasn't doing enough for me, left me caught in a whirlwind of emotions.

When he hung up, he walked into the kitchen and saw me.

"Are you okay, Tyler?" she asked, with that mix of love and concern she usually had.

"I'm fine," I replied, but I knew I wasn't. Not really.

"You have to start taking care of yourself. Not just for yourself, but for us too," he said, his voice a whisper, but I felt the weight of each word.

"I don't need you to take care of me, Mom. I know what I'm doing," I said, feeling my tone turn defensive.

"Really? Do you know?" he asked, and I saw a flash of disappointment in his eyes.

"Yes. Please just leave me alone," I said, and instantly regretted it. The look on his face was heartbreaking, but I didn't know how to take it back.

—Tyler... —she started, but I stopped.

"I can't keep talking about this. I need time," I said, and turned away, leaving her there, lost in her thoughts.

My parents began to ignore me completely, and I responded in kind. We ate at the same table, but as if we were in separate worlds. The atmosphere became thick, and what was once a loving home had become a silent battlefield.

One night, while I was in my room, I heard my mother crying in her room. The sadness emanating from her made me feel a lump in my throat.

I knew that what was happening affected us all. Despite our distance, there was still love. But love was not enough to overcome the barriers we had built for ourselves.

The cycle continued, each doing what they wanted, ignoring the other. Loneliness became a constant in my life, and with each passing day, I felt more lost. No one wanted to acknowledge the situation, and each one wallowed in their own pain, as if it was the only way to deal with the internal storm we all carried.

I wished we could sit down and talk. But every time I tried to open my mouth, I was stopped by the fear of what might come out. The relationship was deteriorating, and even though I knew it, I felt like I couldn't do anything about it.

And so, each day became another struggle. Indifference had settled into our home, and in its place was an emptiness that was as painful as the silence that surrounded it. All I wanted was to go back to the days when laughter filled the corners, and family meals were a chance to bond. But that seemed like a distant dream now, trapped in the fog of what used to be.

Chapter 32

Silence had become a regular companion at home, but it was sometimes interrupted by criticisms from my parents, more like a distant echo than a real conversation. I didn't know how I had gotten to this point, but deep down, I knew there was a chasm between us that grew deeper every day.

It was a Saturday afternoon, and I was in my room, once again scrolling through the beauty products I had ordered online. The image of perfect skin glowed on my laptop screen, and my fingers moved anxiously over the keyboard as I searched for reviews of creams and serums that promised miracles. The obsession had taken a turn I could barely control, but right now, it was the only thing that made me feel like I had any control over my life.

Suddenly, I heard voices in the living room. My parents were arguing again. Normally I tried to ignore their fights, but this time, something about the intensity of their conversation made me pay attention.

"I can't keep watching Tyler like this, obsessing over his appearance," my mother said, the pain in her voice palpable.

"It's just a phase, Claudia. Everyone goes through it," my father replied dismissively. "But what he's doing isn't normal. He needs help."

His tone made my heart race. I couldn't help but feel that his words were a direct criticism towards me, as if they were sentencing me.

"It's not just a phase, David. He's in a dark place, and I don't know how to help him. He's closing himself off more and more and he refuses to talk about what he's feeling," she said, her voice thick with frustration and anguish.

I felt small, trapped in the darkness of my room, like the air had become thick and I had trouble breathing. They didn't understand. They had no idea what it meant to struggle with every mirror I saw, every image of someone I thought was perfect.

I heard my father sigh heavily.

—I've tried. I've tried to talk to him, but he's very tight-lipped. His attitude drives me crazy. —A pause, followed by a softer tone. —Maybe we should talk to a professional.

The thought of a professional sent a chill down my spine. Did they really think I needed help? That my struggle with beauty was so severe that I needed to be brought in to talk about it with a stranger? I couldn't bear the thought.

"I don't know if that will help. What he needs is support, love. But he pulls away. I can't reach him." The vulnerability in my mother's voice made me feel a small flash of guilt, but I quickly smothered it. I couldn't think about that now. I had to protect myself.

I decided it was best to leave my room. I opened the door and, to my surprise, my parents were in the living room, in the middle of a heated conversation. When they saw me, they both fell silent, as if they had been caught in an act they didn't want me to find out about.

"Tyler, do you want to join us?" my mother asked, forcing a smile that didn't reach her eyes.

"No, I'm fine. I just wanted to go out for a while," I replied, trying to keep my voice steady as the lump in my throat grew.

However, my father did not give up.

"Are you sure you're okay? You look more lost than ever, son. What you're doing with your appearance... it's not healthy," he said, his tone sounding critical, judgmental.

I felt like I was being attacked. Rage began to bubble up inside me.

"It's none of your business," I said, trying to contain the explosion of emotions that threatened to overflow.

"It's our business, Tyler. We're watching you fall apart, and I don't know how to help. I see you obsessing over these products and how you look, and it worries me," my mother said, her voice shaking slightly.

"Worry? Really?" I asked, and although I tried to remain calm, the irony made me smile. "Because all they do is criticize me."

BETWEEN PROHIBITIONS AND BINGES   119

"We're not criticizing, we want to help you." My father's voice was firmer now. "But you can't keep going like this."

"Help me? With what? With the same love you have for me while ignoring me at the table? I don't need your help!" I screamed, the words spilling out of my mouth with a rage I didn't know I was building up.

Silence fell over the room. My words seemed to echo off the walls, and even though I knew there had to be some reason for his concern, I felt cornered.

"Tyler, we only want what's best for you," my mother said, her voice soft but filled with sadness. "But I don't understand why you can't see that what you're doing isn't healthy."

That hurt me more than any other comment. I knew they were right, but the truth is I was too caught up in my own mind to consider what they were saying.

"You don't understand. You have no idea what it feels like to be trapped in this. You only see what you want to see. And that's what I'm obsessed with. But you don't understand that it's the only thing I can control," I replied, feeling more lost than ever.

"You're controlling your health, and that's what we're most worried about," my father said, and I saw a flash of concern in his eyes. "If you keep this up, you'll hurt yourself."

It was a low blow. My feelings of guilt and sadness were intertwined with rage.

"Don't talk to me about harm. Have you seen what you say to me? Every comment you make about my weight or my appearance only fuels it more," I said, my words full of venom.

My parents exchanged glances, frustration evident on their faces.

"Tyler, we're not trying to hurt you. We just want you to be happy, to be healthy. But we need you to open up and tell us how you feel," my mother said, and for a moment, her vulnerability made me feel a flicker of empathy. But I quickly smothered it.

"I have nothing to say," I replied, closing the shell tighter than ever.

Without another word, I turned and walked back to my room, closing the door behind me with a slam that echoed down the hall. Tears welled up in my eyes. Loneliness enveloped me like a heavy coat, and I sat up in bed, feeling my chest tighten.

It was an endless cycle. Although the argument had left my parents worried, I became even more withdrawn. Criticism became a constant echo in my mind, feeding the obsession with beauty and the desire for control that had taken hold of me. Sadness became an ally and, at the same time, my jailer.

So there I stood, trapped in the spiral of my thoughts, while life outside continued on without me. No one understood. No one could. The fight was mine, and even if my parents wanted to help, I was too lost in my own labyrinth to let them in.

Chapter 33

The afternoon was cloudy, and the wind blew with a strange force as I decided to go out for a walk. I didn't know why I did it, but there was something about the idea of being alone, away from my parents' criticism, that appealed to me. The path meandered through the park, a place where I used to feel at peace, but today it felt different. Each step led me towards a mix of anxiety and memories that I couldn't avoid.

As I walked, I lost track of time. Leaves crunched under my feet, and loneliness enveloped me like a blanket. At that moment, I thought that maybe I could leave my problems behind, at least for a while. But suddenly, as I turned a corner, I ran into a group of boys from school who had never been nice to me.

"Look who's here!" one of them exclaimed, a mocking laugh echoing through the air. It was Jason, one of my most persistent stalkers.

His words were like a bucket of cold water. A shiver ran through my body, and for a second I was paralyzed. I couldn't believe they had found me here, in this place where I was trying to escape from everything.

"Wow, Tyler. You've lost quite a bit of weight. Are you on a diet or have you just stopped eating?" another said, laughing as he examined me up and down.

The mockery was palpable, and my cheeks burned with shame. I had worked so hard to keep my weight down, and in that moment, bitterness washed over me. It was as if they had come to find me, as if they wanted to assure me that no matter what I did, they would always be there to remind me of what I had been.

"What do they care?" I replied, trying to sound defiant, even though I knew my voice was shaking. "They're not my friends."

"No, but we've always been curious about you," Jason said, crossing his arms, enjoying the attention. "And it seems like your little weight loss project is working. I must admit, you do look... different."

I felt the sarcasm dripping from their words. I didn't know if I should thank them for the "accommodation" or if I should just turn around and walk away. Frustration hit me like a train, and their mockery reminded me that I could never escape what they were.

—Yes, I'm sure I'm 'different' —I said, unable to contain the resentment in my voice—. Is that what you wanted? For me to look the same as all of you, as if what I'm really going through doesn't matter.

"Passing?" Jason laughed again. "Do you really think people care about that? They're just happy to see you lose weight. So instead of complaining, why don't you enjoy it a little more?"

Their words stung. It was a cruel reminder that to them, my suffering was just entertainment. They had seen my struggle as a spectacle, a game in which they won by mocking me, while I sank deeper into my own abyss.

"What about you?" I ventured to ask, feeling the rage welling up in me. "Don't you have anything better to do than torment someone who's already on the ground?"

"We just say what we think, buddy," another of them replied, a boy I barely knew. His tone was dismissive, and I could see the amusement in his eyes.

"What they think doesn't matter. They're just trying to make me feel worse." Desperation washed over me. "Don't they ever get tired of being jerks?"

—That's what makes life interesting. Don't worry, Tyler. We don't care about your life story. At least you look good now. That's all that matters, right?

The hypocrisy was sickening. I realized that even though I tried to brush his comments aside, his attitude had reopened old wounds. My stomach turned, and I wished they would just go away.

BETWEEN PROHIBITIONS AND BINGES   123

"What do you know about my life?" I replied, my words full of bitterness. "You don't know what I've been through. You only see what you want to see."

"Oh, poor thing. Now he's the hero of his own story?" Jason said, his voice thick with contempt. "Maybe you should stop crying over everything and just enjoy the attention. You're on the right track."

I felt a growing rage. I was being mocked and simultaneously reminded that I was trapped in a fight I had never asked for. My thoughts revolved around the idea that their approval was the only thing that mattered, but at the same time, I knew that wasn't true.

"You should be thankful we still notice you," another boy said, as the others laughed. "Last time we saw you, you were a bag of bones. Now, at least, you look human."

The blow was straight to the heart. I tried not to let his words affect me, but deep down, I knew his taunts were aimed at the root of my pain.

"I don't need your validation. I don't care what you think of me," I said, though my voice was shaking. It was a failed attempt at strength, but the truth was that I felt exposed and vulnerable.

"You keep saying that. Maybe one day you'll believe it," Jason replied, with a smile that could have frozen the hottest fire.

After a moment that felt like an eternity, I decided it was best to leave. I didn't want to be a part of his game, I didn't want to be the target of his criticism anymore.

"I don't have time for this," I said, turning on my heel. Every step I took away from them was a small victory. Anger and hurt were mixed together, but at least I was choosing to leave, and that gave me a glimmer of control.

"Take care, Tyler!" Jason shouted behind me, his mocking laughter echoing in the air. "Don't forget to eat something, we don't want you passing out again!"

His words faded into the distance as I walked away, but the echo of his taunt remained in my mind. The mix of emotions was overwhelming: rage, sadness, helplessness. It was a cruel reminder that my fight was not just against my own mind, but also against a world that seemed to delight in my pain.

As I got home, I felt the walls of my room closing in on me once again. The laughter and taunts of my bullies echoed in my mind. I sat up in bed and let the tears fall.

I felt trapped between two worlds: the image I wanted to project and the person I really was. And in between, there was only loneliness.

Chapter 34

The lights in the kitchen are off, and the silence of the house feels like a heavy blanket. It's two in the morning, and everyone is fast asleep. I wake up in the dark, trying to move quietly. My stomach growls and aches, a relentless reminder that it's been empty for days. My footsteps sound like thunder in the hallway, though I know they're just whispers against the floor.

I don't know why I came here. I try to remember the arguments I used to convince myself that I didn't need to eat. There is no food after six, that's the rule, that's the norm I imposed on myself. But tonight, my body doesn't want to listen. Deep down, I feel like I'm losing this battle against hunger, even though I've fought so hard not to give in.

I open the pantry door and my eyes scan the shelves filled with food I should be ignoring. The sight of packets of chips, cookies, and cereal feels like a trap. My fingers move automatically, and before I know it, I have a box of cookies in my hand. Anger and guilt instantly assail me, like I'm doing something unforgivable. I shouldn't be eating, not now. But hunger is like a wave washing over me.

I feel like I'm losing control as I bring one cookie to my mouth, then another, and another. The flavors invade my senses and consume me, just as hunger consumed me. Each bite is a mix of pleasure and regret, of something that comforts me, but at the same time, torments me. The feeling of satisfaction is fleeting, because with each cookie I eat, the guilt grows like a hole in my chest.

"What are you doing, Tyler?" I whisper to myself, trying to stop myself. But I can't, not now.

I don't know how long I spend there, standing, devouring every single thing that comes my way. I don't even think, I just eat and eat, trying to fill a void that seems to have no end. At one point, I start crying. Tears pouring out, one after another, like a cascade of emotions that I can't contain. I feel like a prisoner of my own body, unable to stop this impulse that consumes me.

Finally, when the food is gone and the hunger has been appeased, I realize what I have done. I look at the mess around me: empty wrappers, crumbs on the table, and the feeling of fullness in my stomach that, instead of calming me, makes me hate myself more.

"Why did you do it?" I ask myself, my voice breaking.

I have no answer. I feel the echo of my own words reverberating through the empty kitchen, like a silent accusation. Guilt overwhelms me, and I can't stop thinking about how much I've failed. Everything I've accomplished these past few months, every sacrifice, every day without eating, feels squandered in an instant.

I walk back to my room, but the pain doesn't go away. I crawl into bed and curl up, hoping that sleep will free me from this storm, even though I know that in the morning everything will be worse.

Chapter 35

I can barely sleep after what I did last night. I feel empty, but not from hunger, but from something much worse: shame. I wake up and look at the clock, which reads seven in the morning. I don't want to get up, I don't want to face the day or myself in the mirror. I feel like I'm trapped in a trap with no way out, a routine that consumes me, and the guilt is so intense that I can barely breathe.

When I wake up, the first place I go is the bathroom. I look in the mirror, looking for any changes, any signs of my mistake from last night. But I don't see anything different. Same pale skin, same tired eyes. My stomach still hurts from the amount of food I consumed.

My parents are already awake, and the sound of their voices irritates me. The last thing I want is for them to see me, ask me what's wrong, or worse, mention food.

As I walk into the kitchen, my mother watches me from the table. I feel her gaze, but I don't dare look her in the eyes.

—Did you sleep well? —he asks me.

I nod without saying a word, because I know that if I speak, I will break. I grab a glass of water and drink it slowly, trying to calm the whirlwind inside me.

"You look tired," my father comments, looking at me disapprovingly. He always seems to have something to say about how I look or my decisions.

"I'm fine," I say, my voice sounding raspier than I expected.

"Are you sure?" my mother insists, her tone trying to be gentle, but it only reminds me how little they understand.

"Yes, I'm fine," I repeat curtly, hoping they'll stop asking.

I decide to leave the house before the questions intensify. I don't want to be here, I don't want to face their inquisitive stares and the words that remind me how much I've failed. The memory of last night continues to haunt me, like a shadow I can't shake.

I wander aimlessly through the streets, feeling guilt weighing down my chest. I pass a bakery, and the smell of freshly baked bread makes me feel a mix of craving and disgust. I clench my fists and keep walking, trying to drown out the voice in my head that tells me to eat again.

Finally, I reach a park and sit on a bench. The day is sunny, and I watch people strolling, smiling, enjoying their lives without the burden of this obsession that consumes me. I wonder what it would be like to live without this constant weight on my chest, without this drive that forces me to control every bite, every thought.

I pull out my phone and check my calorie journal, the same ones I had torn up last night in a fit of desperation. I promise myself it won't happen again, that I won't give in to temptation again. But deep down, I know it's an empty promise. This cycle of restriction and guilt feels endless, like there's no escape.

"Why am I like this?" I whisper to myself, my eyes filled with tears. "Why can't I be like everyone else?"

The words hang in the air, but there is no response. I am a prisoner of my own mind, and every attempt to escape only seems to sink me deeper into this abyss of self-loathing.

Chapter 36

The idea began as a whisper. At first, it was a fleeting fantasy, something that crossed my mind without much importance. But over time, it became a constant thought, as if it took root in me and forced me to listen to it.

I look in the mirror, as always, and there it is, the part of my face I hate the most: my nose. It's not that it's monstrous, or that it draws so much attention that it's a cause for ridicule, but to me it's... simply a mistake, something that shouldn't be there. If I could change it, if I could do something to improve it, maybe I would finally see myself in a way that I would accept.

"It shouldn't be that hard," I say to myself quietly, almost as if I were talking to my reflection.

The reflection stares back at me, mockingly. My eyes look tired, the dark circles have become permanent, and the skin I try so hard to take care of doesn't look the way I want it to. None of the creams, soaps, or toners seem to make a difference. I feel like nothing I do can change what I see in the mirror.

The thought of surgery doesn't go away. In the solitude of my room, in the darkest moments, I think about what life would be like if I could reshape my face, if I could build an improved version of myself. In my mind, I imagine myself with a slimmer nose, more defined cheekbones, flawless skin. I imagine what it would be like to wake up every day without feeling ashamed when I look in the mirror.

But the reality is different. I know that surgery is not something I can afford. Even though I wouldn't want to ask my parents for anything, I know that it would be the only way I could afford it. They would never understand. To them, this would be a superficial whim, something unnecessary. But to me, it is something that could change everything.

That night, as I lay in my room, I can't help but search the Internet. "Rhinoplasty," "cosmetic surgery," "improve appearance." I read and read, hours without stopping, as if among the pages of information I could find some magical solution that would allow me to change my life. The before and after pictures of patients fascinate me; I see how normal, even ordinary people manage to transform themselves into versions that seem almost unreal.

"Why can't I have that?" I ask myself quietly, feeling envy and desperation rising inside me.

I turn off the computer and lie down on my bed, staring at the ceiling. I know it's just a fantasy, something I'll probably never achieve, but in the back of my mind the thought keeps repeating: someday. Someday, I'll change who I am, I'll become a better person.

Chapter 37

The days go by and my obsession grows. Every time I see someone on the street with a perfect nose or flawless skin, my self-hatred intensifies. I wonder if I can ever be like them, if I will ever stop feeling trapped in this body I hate.

Today, in English class, I can't concentrate. The teacher is talking about grammar, but my mind is elsewhere. I'm thinking about the surgeries I've seen, the testimonies of people who claim their lives changed after having surgery. I hear them in my head, as if they were calling me, as if they were promising me a better life.

Suddenly, I notice the teacher looking at me.

—Tyler, are you okay? —she asks, with a worried expression.

I nod quickly, trying not to look out of place.

—Yeah, I was just... thinking.

She smiles at me, but I don't think she understands what's really going on with me. No one understands. When class is over, I decide to walk around a bit. I need to clear my head, but every person I see on the street seems to have something I don't have. A girl with a perfect nose, a man with a strong, defined jaw. They all seem better than me, more complete, more worth looking at.

When I get home, my parents are in the living room. I look at my father and think about what it would look like if I had his facial structure. Maybe with a jaw like his, I would look more masculine, more attractive.

I don't say anything, but they notice my presence.

"Are you okay, son?" my mother asks, with a slight smile.

I nod again, pretending everything is okay.

I go up to my room and close the door, feeling frustration building in my chest. I lie down on the bed and close my eyes, allowing myself to dream once more. I imagine what it would be like to have a perfect nose, higher cheekbones, flawless skin. In my mind, I am someone different, someone who could finally be happy.

But reality hits me hard. It's just a dream, a fantasy that I'll never be able to fulfill.

Chapter 38

I haven't been able to sleep well for days. Every time I close my eyes, my mind is filled with images of myself with a new face, a different appearance. I wake up sweating, feeling like I'm trapped in a body that isn't mine.

My parents begin to notice that something is wrong with me. My mother approaches me one day in the kitchen, while I am preparing a glass of water.

—Tyler, are you sure you're okay? You look worried.

I look at her and for a moment, I want to tell her everything. I want to tell her that I hate the way I look, that I dream of changing my appearance, that it hurts to see my own reflection every day. But I know she wouldn't understand.

—I'm fine, I just have things on my mind.

She nods, even though I know she's not convinced. She takes a sigh and looks at me, as if she wants to say something more, but in the end she decides to stay silent.

That afternoon, I decide to walk alone to the park. The cold air clears my head a little, but my mind is still tormented. I see a couple walking hand in hand, both laughing, both... perfect. I wonder if anyone will ever see me that way, if anyone could ever fall in love with someone like me.

I reach a bench and sit down, head in hands. I close my eyes and try to calm down, but the thought of surgery is still there, like a constant whisper in my mind.

"Why do I have to be like this?" I mutter to myself, feeling the tears building up in my eyes.

The answer never comes. No one can give me a reason. All I know is that I don't want to go on like this, that I don't want to live trapped in a body I hate.

Finally, as night falls, I get up and start walking back home. I feel the cold on my face, but I barely notice it. I'm so wrapped up in my thoughts that I almost don't notice when I reach my front door.

My parents are already asleep when I get in. I go up to my room and look at myself in the mirror once more. There it is, the same old face, the same appearance I detest. I feel the rage and frustration burning inside me, as if my own reflection were a mockery.

"Someday," I whisper, my tone determined.

Someday, I promise myself, I will change who I am.

Chapter 39

Every day seems to start out worse than the last. I wake up feeling like I haven't slept in weeks, my muscles are weak, and I feel a heaviness that goes beyond the physical. I feel exhausted, but I ignore it. The pain and fatigue are insignificant compared to the satisfaction of watching my body continue to change.

Today, however, as I look in the mirror, I notice something different: small strands of hair in the sink. I stare at it for a moment, trying not to think about what it means, but deep down, I feel a twinge of alarm. I run a hand through my hair and notice that it seems thinner, less dense. My fingers easily find the scalp, and suddenly, insecurity and fear begin to creep into my mind.

"It doesn't matter," I tell myself quietly, forcing a smile that I barely feel. I tell myself that it's a small price to pay, that losing a little hair is nothing compared to the goal I have in mind. But, as much as I try to convince myself, something inside me begins to doubt.

During the day, fatigue never leaves me. When I try to get up from my chair, I feel a dizziness that makes me stagger. I hold on to the edge of the table and close my eyes, waiting for it to pass.

"Are you okay?" my mother asks, looking at me from the doorway with concern.

I look at her and fake a smile, even though I feel like I'm on the verge of collapsing.

—Yeah, I'm just a little tired. It's school... you know, homework and all that —I say quickly, trying to sound convincing.

She frowns at me, but eventually nods, though she doesn't seem entirely convinced.

—Maybe you should get more rest... —he suggests quietly, before turning to leave the room.

"Rest more." The words ring hollow in my mind. There is no time to rest, I can't lose focus. Every sacrifice, every feeling of weakness, is

135

worth it. I remind myself that this is temporary, that at some point I will see the results I desire.

At night, I lie in bed and close my eyes, trying to ignore the pain in my abdomen. My stomach hasn't been feeling right for weeks; sometimes, it feels like everything I eat falls on me like a rock. Even the few foods I do eat make me uncomfortable. But I remind myself again that it doesn't matter, that every discomfort is one step closer to the slimness I so crave.

Just as I begin to fall asleep, I feel a tear slide down my cheek. I don't know where it comes from, I don't know why I'm crying, but the pain in my chest becomes unbearable, as if all the effort, all the fatigue and loneliness are beginning to take their toll on me.

Chapter 40

I wake up with a stabbing pain in my stomach, like something is tearing me apart from the inside. I struggle to get up, but my legs barely respond. I feel like I'm carrying the weight of a mountain on my back.

As I pass the bathroom, I notice hairs in the sink again. This time, there seem to be a lot more of them, and I feel my heart racing. I run my hands through my hair again and feel it tangle around my fingers, as if my own body is falling apart.

"Everything is fine," I tell myself, though I'm not so sure anymore. I walk to the kitchen, where my mother is preparing breakfast. The smell is nauseating, as if my stomach can't handle it.

"Are you going to eat something?" he asks me, without looking at me.

"I'm not hungry," I reply, almost automatically.

She sighs and turns around, looking at me with a mix of concern and frustration.

—Tyler, you need to eat. You can't keep skipping meals. You're... you're getting paler, and your eyes... —she shakes her head, as if she doesn't want to finish the sentence.

"I'm fine, Mom," I say, trying to sound firm. "I'm just a little tired."

She doesn't seem convinced, but she doesn't push it either. I turn and walk out of the kitchen before she can say anything else. I walk toward the park, trying to clear my head. But with every step, the weakness becomes more apparent. My legs shake and the pain in my abdomen intensifies.

Finally, I sit down on a bench and take a deep breath, trying to calm the discomfort. All around me, people pass by, unconcerned, as if I didn't exist, as if my pain were invisible. I close my eyes and let the sun caress my face, trying to find some comfort in the warmth, even if it's just for a moment.

137

When I open my eyes, I see a girl sitting on a nearby bench, looking away. She has short hair, and she looks as fragile as I feel. Our eyes meet for a moment, and I wonder if she is going through something similar, if she also feels this emptiness, this loneliness that seems to eat me up from within.

Suddenly, I feel a pressure on my chest, as if the weight of everything I'm doing is becoming unbearable. Tears begin to fall uncontrollably, and I can't stop them. I lower my head, trying to hide them, ashamed of my weakness.

"Are you okay?" the girl asks me, with a soft voice that almost makes me feel like someone understands me.

I nod quickly, without raising my head.

—Yes... I'm just... I'm just tired.

She doesn't say anything, but she just stands there, silent, as if she understands without words. I'd like to tell her everything, tell her about my pain, about my obsession, about how my body seems to be betraying me. But I can't. I don't know how.

Finally, I get up and walk back home, shuffling my feet, feeling like every step is a struggle. When I arrive, my mother is in the living room, looking at me with concern.

"Tyler?" she calls. "Please take care of yourself."

I look at her, unable to answer, and go up to my room. I sit on the bed and look at myself in the mirror. My reflection reflects back an image I barely recognize: pale, weak, tired. But despite everything, my mind remains obsessed with thinness. I remind myself that this is what I want, that I am closer than ever to achieving my goal.

But deep down, a part of me starts to question it. At what cost? How much more can I take?

Chapter 41

The nights are getting longer and longer. I find it hard to close my eyes and find rest. My thoughts swirl around in my head, like an endless echo that haunts me, tormenting me. I am exhausted, but it seems that not even sleep can give me relief. And when I finally do, I wake up with the same empty feeling.

Today, after only a few hours of sleep, I wake up and look in the mirror. I don't recognize myself. My skin is pale, my eyes sunken and surrounded by dark shadows. I feel like a stranger in my own body. It's like I've blurred, like every part of me is made of smoke, about to disappear. But deep down, a voice keeps telling me that I have to keep going, that it's not enough yet.

I go down to the kitchen, and my parents are already eating breakfast. They look at me, but they don't say anything. I wonder if they see what I see, if they notice that something in me is broken. They don't mention anything, though. It seems like everyone has learned to keep quiet, to pretend that everything is okay, even when it clearly isn't.

"Aren't you going to eat anything?" my mother asks, breaking the silence.

—I'm not hungry —I answer automatically.

My father snorts and stirs his coffee. He doesn't say anything, but his expression says it all. He's tired of my excuses, of seeing me as I am, or maybe of pretending to care. Maybe he's tired of me too, like I am of myself.

I go up to my room, unable to bear the tension in the air. I sit on my bed and let the silence envelop me. I try to gather my thoughts, to make some sense of it all, but I feel completely lost. I don't know who I am or what I'm doing. I look in the mirror, searching for answers, but all I see is an empty image. There's nothing.

Chapter 42

The days pass in a blur, and I continue to function on automatic. I go to school, I come back, I avoid my parents, I avoid everyone. I feel trapped in some kind of limbo, disconnected from everything, like I'm floating in a thick fog that prevents me from seeing clearly. Everything seems foreign to me. Other people's words sound distant, as if they come from another world. Even my own voice seems strange to me.

One day at school, while I was in class, a classmate approached me.

"Are you okay?" he asks me, and I can see a mix of concern and curiosity on his face.

I look at him, not knowing what to say. I really don't know. I'm not okay, but I'm not bad either. I'm... empty.

"Yeah, I'm fine," I finally reply, though it sounds like a lie even to me.

He nods, but he doesn't seem convinced. He watches me for a moment, as if he's trying to see through my facade, but eventually he turns and walks away. I stand there, staring at the empty space he left, wondering if I'll ever feel anything other than this indifference, this disconnection again.

That night, as I try to sleep, I find myself crying silently. I don't know why. There's no specific reason. I just feel like something in me is broken, something I can't fix. I hug myself, as if that will make the pain go away, but it's no use. Sadness is like a shadow enveloping me, suffocating me.

Chapter 43

Things at home aren't getting any better. My parents barely speak to me, and when they do, it's to criticize my decisions, to question my habits, to remind me that I'm not enough. The pressure of their disapproval adds to the burden I carry inside, and I feel like I'm on the verge of breaking.

One day, while I am in the living room, my father calls me.

—Tyler, can you come here for a moment?

I walk over, trying to prepare myself for whatever he has to say to me. I know it won't be good.

"What is this?" she asks, pointing to a bag full of beauty products on the table.

Those products... I bought them with the little money I had left, hoping that somehow they could help me feel better. But now, looking at them through their eyes, I feel ridiculous, as if all those jars and creams were a reflection of my desperation.

—It's just... things I need, —I answer quietly, avoiding his gaze.

"Do you need this?" he repeats, disdainfully. "You spend money on nonsense, instead of worrying about important things. Do you think this is going to solve anything? Do you think it will change who you are?"

His words hit me like a punch in the stomach. I try not to show it, but I feel my chest filling with anger and sadness.

—You don't understand... —I murmur, almost in a whisper.

"You're right, I don't understand," he replies coldly. "I don't understand why you're so obsessed with your appearance. Maybe if you put that effort into something that really matters, you could accomplish something."

I can't take it anymore. I feel like I'm about to explode. Tears start to well up in my eyes, and I turn away before he can see them.

141

"You have no idea how I feel," I say, my voice shaking with frustration. "You have no idea how hard it is for me... every day."

He doesn't answer. He just stands there, staring at me indifferently, and that's what hurts the most. The indifference, the lack of understanding. It's like I'm a stranger in my own home, like my problems are invisible to them.

I go up to my room and slam the door shut. I sit on the bed and hug my knees, trying to hold back my tears, but it's impossible. I feel like I'm falling apart, like every part of me is breaking down into tiny, irreparable pieces.

I stand there, silent, in the dark, feeling more alone than ever. No one understands what I'm going through. No one sees the pain I carry inside.

Chapter 44

I remember times when the air was just air and not this suffocating burden I feel in my chest. There was a time in my life, so long ago, when I used to feel... free. Yes, that's the word: free. I could walk without being aware of every glance, without thinking about the weight of every step, every imperfection on my skin. It was as if this emptiness inside me didn't exist, as if I could breathe deeply without being suffocated.

One of those times was during the summers when I would go to my grandparents' house. I remember one day in particular; I was eight or nine years old and my grandfather had taken me to a lake that was quite far away. The two of us were driving in silence, just the sound of the tires on the dirt road and the wind coming through the windows. I remember the radio was broken, and instead of songs, we heard the breeze and the rustling of tree branches as they passed by.

"You know, Tyler," he said, breaking the silence, "there are times when you just need to disconnect from everything so you can listen to what you have inside."

"And what's inside?" I asked, not quite understanding.

"You'll find out, son. But when you find out, don't let anyone take it away from you," he replied, with a smile that was all confidence.

I didn't fully understand those words at the time, but they stick in my head now. Because I think that somewhere along the line in my life, I let something—or someone—take that part of me away from me. Maybe it was the years at school, the teasing, the stares that focused on every little thing about me that didn't fit their ideals. Maybe it was the time at home, where every choice I made always seemed insufficient to my parents, every effort overshadowed by some criticism, some comparison to others.

That afternoon at the lake was special. I jumped into the water without a second thought, feeling the freshness cover my skin, the rays of sunlight reflecting off the surface, my grandfather's laughter echoing in the air. Everything was simple, without worries, without the need to be anything other than myself.

But now... now I'm trapped in a prison of my own making. Every thought is a cell, every insecurity a lock. I look in the mirror and see only the flaws, the mistakes, the things I hate about myself. It's like that boy laughing in the lake has disappeared, like he never existed.

Chapter 45

I think of another, more recent memory. It was a few years ago, before all this obsession started. My parents had had a big fight, and I, feeling trapped in the tense atmosphere of the house, decided to go for a walk. I found a small hill behind our neighborhood and climbed to the top. I remember the tiredness in my legs, the sweat on my forehead, but also the peace when I got to the top and saw the view. From there I could see the whole neighborhood, the lights of the houses twinkling in the distance.

I lay down on the ground and let the sky become my roof, the cold of the night caress my skin. I felt, even if only for a moment, that the world was immense, that there was so much to explore, so many possibilities to be myself without limits, without judgment. In that moment, I allowed myself to dream of a life in which I was not constantly worried about my appearance, a life in which every decision was not conditioned by the fear of disappointing someone.

But those moments are gone now. Now, when I try to find peace, I only find more pressure, more demands. It's like every corner of my mind is occupied by a critical voice that never shuts up. No matter how hard I try, no matter how many times I try to convince myself that I'm enough, that voice is always there, telling me otherwise.

And I'm so tired... So tired of living with this burden, of waking up every morning and feeling like every step is a monumental effort. The people around me don't even notice. To them, I'm just Tyler, the boy who tries his best to fit in, who tries to live up to expectations. They don't know that behind every smile is a torrent of self-doubt, that every word I say is carefully calculated to not give too much away.

Sometimes I wonder what would have happened if I had never let those comments affect me, if I could have continued being that boy at the lake, or the teenager on the hill, without the weight of approval, without the pressure of being something I don't even understand. But it's too late. Now I'm here, a prisoner of myself, in a place I don't know how to escape.

Chapter 46

The thought of getting out of bed has become an unbearable weight. I open my eyes every morning, feeling as if the world is closing in on me, as if each day is a challenge I don't want to face. Before, even when things were going badly, there were small moments that gave me some comfort: a sunny afternoon, listening to music, reading a book. Now, none of it makes sense. It's as if everything that used to make me feel something is now just a shadow, an empty echo of something that is no longer there.

I get up and walk around the house aimlessly, avoiding any contact. My parents barely see me, and if they do, we simply exchange cold glances, laden with everything we never say to each other. I become enraged once again by this silence that has become our routine, in this house that now feels like a prison.

Today I try to remember a time when I was truly happy. My thoughts take me back, but even those memories are clouded, distorted by the way I see myself now. All I can think about are the things I've done wrong, the times I've failed. The happy memories seem to be of someone else, someone I'm no longer, someone I may never have been.

I keep avoiding my reflection in mirrors. I don't want to face what I see, because every time I do, I hate myself more. It's a constant war between what I am and what I want to be, a fight I always lose. Every time I avoid looking at myself, I think of all the flaws I imagine others see, of all the unspoken comments hidden behind the gazes of those I pass.

Chapter 47

The few times I make the effort to leave my room, everything seems grayer, duller. It's like the whole world is shrouded in a fog that separates me from everyone else. I walk down the streets feeling invisible, as if I'm in another dimension. I see people laughing, talking, living their lives, and I realize how detached I feel from all of that. There's an invisible wall between me and them, a barrier I don't know how to break down.

I haven't talked to anyone beyond the essentials in weeks. My friends stopped asking me out, I guess because I always found some excuse. Deep down, they must be fed up with me too, tired of my constant negativity, of this broken version of someone they used to know. I don't blame them. I'd be tired of myself too if I were them.

One day, my mother tries to talk to me in the kitchen. She's making dinner, and I'm there, pretending to be looking for something in the pantry just so I don't have to look directly at her.

"Tyler..." she starts, her voice trying to be nice but not sounding genuine. I can almost feel her discomfort, like she doesn't know what words to choose to reach me. "I haven't seen you hanging out with your friends lately. Are you okay?"

"Yes, Mom," I reply, without even looking up. "I'm just... tired, that's all."

"You have to understand that locking yourself away isn't going to make you feel better, Tyler," she says, trying to sound wise. But all I hear in her words is reproach, one more expectation I can't meet.

"I know, Mom," I repeat, a little colder than I should. "But... right now it's what I need."

She sighs, and even though I can't look at her, I can imagine the frustration on her face. I know she would like me to be different, to be the son she always imagined, someone happy, confident. But that son doesn't exist. It's just me, with all my imperfections, my failures.

148

BETWEEN PROHIBITIONS AND BINGES

After a few minutes, she leaves the kitchen without saying anything else, leaving me there, in that silence that seems to consume everything. The truth is, I don't even know how to express what I feel. I want to tell her that I'm lost, that I don't know how to get out of this dark place I'm in, but the words don't come out, and instead, I'm just left with that weight on my chest, that sinking feeling that seems to never go away.

Sometimes I wonder how much longer I can bear this burden.

Chapter 48

I look in the mirror like I have so many times before, hoping to find something, anything to tell me that this all makes sense, that I have arrived somewhere. But what I see is a stranger, someone trapped in a body that is never enough, in a war that seems to have no end. The truth is that I see only flaws, imperfections everywhere: the face that is sharp but not yet "perfect," the skin that has not quite healed, the shadows under my eyes that reveal how exhausted I am.

"What do you want?" I ask myself, searching for an answer in my reflection.

Sometimes I realize that this obsession is no longer normal. What I feel is something darker, deeper, like an abyss that consumes me every day. Is this what body dysmorphia feels like? Everything in me tells me that I am not enough, that I still see myself as too big, too imperfect, even though others tell me otherwise. This obsession drags me down and won't leave me alone. I know I have anorexia, even though I hate that word, I hate everything it implies. Because the last thing I want is to have a "problem" or appear weak.

My breathing quickens as I run my shaking hands over my stomach and arms, searching for any sign that all this sacrifice has paid off. All I feel is that it's not enough, that I'm still far from being someone worthwhile.

I'd like to get these thoughts out of my mind, to erase once and for all those looks, the laughs and the comments from people who told me I wasn't good enough. But it's all etched into my skin, in every corner of my mind, like a voice that never stops.

—You're just a boy with body dysmorphia and anorexia... —I whisper, as if saying it out loud could relieve some of this weight.

But the reflection doesn't respond; it gives me back the same broken image of someone who doesn't know how to feel good about

BETWEEN PROHIBITIONS AND BINGES

themselves. Maybe admitting it out loud makes me seem more aware, but in reality I feel trapped, as if this is all a trap I can't escape from.

I close my eyes and try to imagine a version of myself that doesn't have to deal with this, someone who can look in the mirror and feel at peace, but the image fades away in seconds. I can't hold on to it. It's gone as quickly as it came, leaving me alone, in this familiar darkness.

Then the truth hits me hard: all this fighting, this obsession with my appearance, with becoming "better," is just an illusion. I've been chasing something unattainable, something I can never reach, because there will always be something I don't like, there will always be a critic or a voice telling me I'm not enough yet. I'm just a kid trapped in this prison of my own making, a place filled with criticism, impossible expectations, and a dissatisfaction that won't let me go.

Tears begin to fall as I continue to stare at my reflection. I feel broken, like I'm beyond repair, and as much as I want to find some way to fix myself, I know it won't be easy.

Chapter 49

Pain is a constant companion. It has become part of my routine, like waking up in the morning or feeling the cold air on my skin. The pressure in my chest and the constant uneasiness in my stomach remind me that I am alive, but not in the way I want to be. Sometimes, I wish physical pain was all I felt. But what really consumes me is the tumult in my mind, that endless battle between who I am and who I long to be.

I wake up and look at myself in the mirror. The reflection stares back at me defiantly. My eyes, sunken and tired, meet a face that seems foreign to me. I have been controlling every bite, every calorie, as if that gave me some kind of power. But at the same time, that struggle has taken me to a dark place, where physical suffering is intertwined with emotional suffering.

"What happened to you?" I wonder out loud, as if I could find some answer.

I get out of the shower and put on my clothes, the same old clothes, the ones that don't fit perfectly but at least allow me to avoid being criticized. Each item of clothing is a battle; every time I put it on, I'm determined to fight against what I see, against the image reflected in the mirror. But deep down, I know I can't go on like this. There is a limit, and I'm crossing boundaries I never thought I would reach.

I decide to skip breakfast. My parents call me from the kitchen, asking if I'm going to join them.

"I'm not hungry," I reply, my tone sounding colder than I intended. I really don't want to deal with their worried looks or their questions about my health.

"Tyler, you need to eat something," my mother insists, her voice full of concern.

"I'm fine, really," my reply is a whisper. But deep down, I know it's not true. I've never been so far from fine.

BETWEEN PROHIBITIONS AND BINGES

I leave the house, leaving my parents behind, whispering worries I can't bear to hear. I walk aimlessly, feeling the cold air embrace me. With every step, I cling to the idea that if I'm thinner, everything will be better. That idea has become my mantra, but it's an illusion that consumes me.

Physical pain is easier to bear. I find myself in a park, watching others enjoy the day. They laugh, play, share moments that seem so simple, so innocent. I envy that freedom, that lack of concern for appearance. Yet the idea of giving up the fight scares me even more than the pain I feel. What would happen if I gave up on all this? What would be left of me?

My mind wanders to dark thoughts. Images of myself, too big, too flaccid, fill my mind. The stabbing pain in my stomach screams at me that I am doing the right thing by avoiding food. But at what cost? The hands of my family trying to help me are just a reminder of what I cannot be.

"I just need to keep going like this," I whisper to myself as I clutch my stomach, as if I can remember the empty feeling that a false sense of control gives me.

Suddenly, I feel the urge to eat, hunger hitting me with a force I can't ignore. However, instead of satisfying that need, I look for a nearby coffee shop. My body moves by inertia, while in my mind I repeat to myself that I can't eat. When I arrive, I order a coffee, just that. Just a liquid, without calories to ruin my day.

As I wait, I watch the people passing by. They seem happy, carefree. In their world, they don't have to fight their reflection every morning, they don't have to fight the voice that screams at them that they're never good enough. I feel a pang in my heart. Why can't I be like them?

I sit and stare out the window. Tears begin to pool in my eyes. I can't go on like this, but I don't know how to stop. Every time I promise myself that today will be different, that promise fades away, taking any glimmer of hope with it.

I sit in my chair, feeling like time is standing still. People are coming in and out, but I'm trapped in this bubble of sadness. Then hunger becomes a monster in my stomach, roaring and threatening to break the thin line I've drawn.

When the coffee finally arrives, I look at it as if it's the only solace I have left. I take a sip, the warm liquid momentarily easing the emptiness, but at the same time, filling me with guilt. I imagine myself sitting in my room, my parents knocking on the door, wondering what's wrong with me. Will they ever know the torment I carry inside?

I decide to leave the café and head back home, my thoughts growing darker. As I walk, the internal struggle intensifies. In my mind, a cry grows louder: "Why can't you just be happy?"

Physical and mental pain takes hold of me, like a shadow that won't let me escape. Despite this, I continue to cling to my destructive habits, searching for relief that never comes. The cycle of restriction and self-criticism repeats itself, and each day is a more exhausting struggle than the last.

Finally, I get home and lock myself in my room. I want to scream, I want to cry, but all I can do is stay silent, trapped in my own mind. As the pain consumes me, I cling to the one thing I think defines me: my struggle to be thinner, to be "better."

But at the same time, I wonder if I will ever be able to bear this pain anymore. Life has become an endless cycle of suffering and unfulfilled longings.

I collapse onto the bed, the tears begin to flow, but at the same time I feel lost in an ocean of sadness. What path should I follow? The struggle continues, but with each step, I feel like I'm sinking a little deeper, as if I were caught in a current that doesn't let me breathe.

Life goes on, but here I am, stuck, wishing I could find a way out of this nightmare.

Chapter 50

The afternoon had been particularly tense. Ever since I woke up, the atmosphere at home had been charged, as if a storm was brewing on the horizon. My parents exchanged worried glances, whispering to each other about things I couldn't hear, but which clearly included me. Still, the notion that they might try to take me to a mental institution had never crossed my mind.

I sat on the couch, feeling the pressure in my chest increasing. I tried to concentrate on a series that was playing, but the voices of the characters were just background noise. My mind was caught in a spiral of dark thoughts. The idea of being "normal" seemed increasingly distant. The hunger, the emptiness, the struggle... Everything had become like a second skin.

"Tyler, we need to talk," my mother said, her voice shaking slightly. I turned to look at her. Her face was filled with concern, but also a determination I hadn't seen before.

"About what?" I asked, trying to remain as nonchalant as possible. Deep down, I knew it wasn't a good sign.

"We... think you need professional help," my father said, with a seriousness that made me feel like I'd been punched in the stomach.

"Professional help?" I repeated, in disbelief. The thought of being taken to a mental hospital filled me with panic.

—Tyler, this isn't a game. We've seen how you've been and... —my mother tried to come closer, but I backed away, as if her hand was on fire.

"I don't need help. I'm not crazy," I replied, raising my voice. Frustration was consuming me. How could they think I was crazy for wanting to control my body?

"That's not what we're saying," my father said, but his tone was firm, almost authoritative. "We're worried about your health. We haven't seen you eat properly in weeks. You're losing weight and you look... you look sick."

"I'm not sick!" I cried, feeling the tears begin to well up. Anger and sadness mixed in an explosion of emotions that I could barely control.

"What you're doing to yourself is not healthy, Tyler," my mother insisted, her voice shaking slightly. "We want to help you."

Rage boiled inside me. Help? What kind of help were they talking about? Help meant giving up, it meant accepting that I needed someone to fix me. And that was the last thing I wanted. The thought of being taken to a place where I would have no control over my life filled me with terror.

"I'm not going," I said, my voice low but determined.

My father exchanged a glance with my mother, and suddenly the tension in the air became tangible. I could see that they were willing to do something I didn't want to. My heart was pounding, adrenaline was beginning to course through my veins.

—Tyler, this is for your own good. —My mother's words sounded more like an ultimatum.

"No!" I replied, getting up from the couch. My body was shaking with frustration. "They won't take me anywhere!"

I tried to leave the room, but my parents blocked my way. Desperation turned to fear, and fear to anger.

—We can't keep watching you hurt yourself. —My father stared at me, as if he was trying to get inside my head.

"I'm not hurting anyone. I'm just a boy who wants to be thin!" I screamed, feeling my voice echoing off the walls. I couldn't believe this was happening. It was like a bad dream I couldn't wake up from.

"Tyler, we can't let this continue," my mother said, tears in her eyes. Her expression broke me inside, but my resolve didn't waver.

At that moment, I decided I wasn't going to let them take me. My mind was racing. I pushed my father away with all my strength and ran to my room. I slammed the door shut, listening to the impact echo through the house. The sound of my heart pounding in my ears.

"Tyler, open the door!" my mother screamed, her voice filled with anguish.

—No, leave me alone! —I replied, feeling despair overwhelm me.

I began searching for something to block the door. I couldn't let them in. I didn't want to be taken to that place. My hands shook as I searched for a chair to prop against the door. I felt like I was caught in a battle I didn't want to be a part of, and every passing second filled me with more fear.

—Please, Tyler, we just want to help you. —My father's voice echoed from the other side of the door, his tone calmer, but there was no way he could fool me.

"Help me?" I replied, scornfully. "Help me lose what little control I have? No!"

The door shook slightly as my mother tried to open it. My heart was racing, and I felt a mixture of anxiety and crushing sadness. It was as if the room was closing in on me.

"You're not alone in this," my father said, his voice breaking. "We're here for you."

But that wasn't true. It felt like they were fighting against me, rather than standing beside me. The fight I had inside of me wasn't something I could share. It was a monster I had created and nurtured for years. And now, I couldn't let them take it away from me.

—No! I don't want help! —I screamed, letting the rage escape me in the form of tears.

And so, as I listened to their desperate voices on the other side of the door, I felt loneliness engulf me, heavier than ever. It was an endless cycle, a dead end. I knew I should open the door, that I should let my parents in, but in my mind, that door had become the only barrier protecting me.

The sound of his hands pounding on the door echoed in my head, and as the tears took over me, the truth became clear. At that moment, I was more alone than ever.

Pain, fear and despair tangled together in a whirlwind as I sank deeper into darkness. "Would this be the end of my fight?" The only answer I had was the echo of their voices, and deep inside, I knew I wouldn't open the door.

Chapter 51

The desperate sound of knocking on the door made me shiver. "Tyler, please let us in," my mother's voice said, laced with an anguish she had never meant to cause. I felt my heart pounding in my chest, a constant reminder of the reality around me. I knew they were worried, but that worry felt like a prison, a chain keeping me tied to a life I didn't want.

I stood in the corner of my room, fighting the urge to open the door. "I don't want to talk," I muttered, even though I knew they couldn't hear me. The words were just an echo in my mind, resonating with the frustration of days, weeks, months of isolation. The thought of facing their disappointment filled me with a fear that was hard to bear.

"We're not angry, son," my father interjected, his tone softer now. "We just want to help you. Please open the door for us."

The pressure in my chest increased. They only wanted to help, but they didn't understand that their help felt like an invasion, as if every piece of advice and concern was another layer of my prison. "I don't need help," I replied quietly, but the echo of my voice was lost in the silence that followed.

I dropped to the floor, my back pressed against the cold wood. The room was dark, and memories of previous arguments flooded my mind. Every time I tried to open up, every time I shared a fragment of what I was feeling, it ended in another confrontation, another loss of connection. The thought of opening the door now seemed overwhelming.

My mind began to wander to the days when I felt free. I remembered moments in the park, laughing with friends, running without a goal in mind, enjoying life as it was. But those moments seemed so far away, as if they belonged to another person, to another time. The daily struggle to fit in, to be accepted, had consumed me.

"Tyler, please," my mother pleaded, her voice breaking. "We can't help you if you don't let us in."

159

I felt like a part of me wanted to open that door, but the other part refused to budge. The internal struggle made me feel more alone than ever. "Why can't they understand that I can't do this?" I thought as a tear rolled down my cheek.

My mind filled with images of my parents looking at me with disappointment, of the times I had failed to meet their expectations. Their words echoed in my head: "You look so thin, are you okay?" And I could only smile with a sadness they didn't see, because in their world, thinness was synonymous with success.

"Come on, Tyler, just once," my father insisted. "Remember the last time we did this together? We need to talk."

The memory of her hit me like a wave. It had been so long ago. Before this struggle became my only reality. "I don't want to remember," I murmured, but nostalgia washed over me, and sadness grew in my chest.

Instead of opening the door, I crept to the mirror once more. The image I saw stared back at me, and a deep sense of disappointment washed over me. The evening light filtered through the window, illuminating the contours of my figure, but all I saw was emptiness. My skin was pale and my gaze dull, as if the life had faded from me.

"You are a failure," I whispered, feeling the sting of tears in my eyes. "You will never be enough."

At that moment, I realized that I wasn't just fighting my self-image; I was fighting expectations, memories of ridicule, and the overwhelming desire to be accepted. My mind filled with dark thoughts, and despair gripped me like a monster I couldn't control.

—Tyler, please, we just want to know that you're safe —my mother insisted again, and I felt her anguish palpable, like a thread that tied me to the reality I was trying to escape.

"I'm safe," I replied, but the words rang hollow even to me. Was I really safe? Or was I just hiding my pain? The struggle to be thin had taken over my life, each day a new reminder that I could never be enough.

"We love you, son. We can't stand by and watch you hurt yourself," my father said, concern evident in his tone.

Instead of opening the door, I dropped back to the floor, tears flowing uncontrollably. "I'm not hurting anyone," I cried, even though I knew it wasn't true. The truth was, I was hurting myself, and I knew it. But opening the door meant facing the pain and disappointment I'd been avoiding.

"Tyler, listen to me," my mother said, her voice shaking. "We're here for you. We always will be. But we can't help you if you don't let us in."

The words hung in the air, and I felt helpless. The battle inside me intensified. The fight to remain the skinny kid, the kid who fit in, became a chain heavier than any I had ever carried.

"I don't know what to do," I murmured, and at that moment, I realized that it was not only a cry of anguish, but a cry for help.

But the shadows of my thoughts were more powerful than the desire to open the door. So I stayed there, trapped in my room, staring blankly into the mirror and the struggle in my heart. The sound of my parents continued to echo at the door, their love and concern crashing against the wall of my isolation.

Finally, I gave in to the sadness that enveloped me. I looked in the mirror once more, searching for something that would give me hope, something that would make me feel like I could find a way out. But all I saw was an endless struggle, a cycle that didn't seem to have an end.

And so, there I was, in the silence of my room, with the echo of their voices resonating in my mind, facing the harsh reality of my life. The door was still closed, and I was still trapped in a labyrinth from which I didn't know how to escape.

MAURICIO ABAN

END.

About the Author

Mauricio Aban es un escritor argentino conocido por sus obras publicadas en la plataforma de Wattpad. Su estilo versátil abarca una variedad de géneros, incluyendo acción, romance, misterio y terror. Aban es reconocido por su enfoque poco convencional, ya que sus historias raramente concluyen con finales felices, reflejando su visión de la complejidad de la vida real. Explorando las complejidades de la existencia, Aban crea tramas inmersivas que desafían las expectativas de los lectores. A pesar de su inclinación hacia finales menos convencionales, sus obras continúan atrayendo a los lectores, ofreciendo un emocionante escape de la realidad. Como escritor en constante evolución, Aban busca conectar con los lectores a través de narrativas cautivadoras que invitan a la reflexión sobre la condición humana. Su objetivo es proporcionar una experiencia literaria que entretenga y ofrezca un escape para aquellos que buscan explorar mundos fuera de lo común.

Read more at https://www.wattpad.com/_uname=mauricioban3.